COVEN OF THE EAST

Reimagining Asian Women's Magical Histories

Edited by

ANGELA YURIKO SMITH

Edited by

PAULINE CHOW

Authortunities Press & Ghastly Goings-On Press

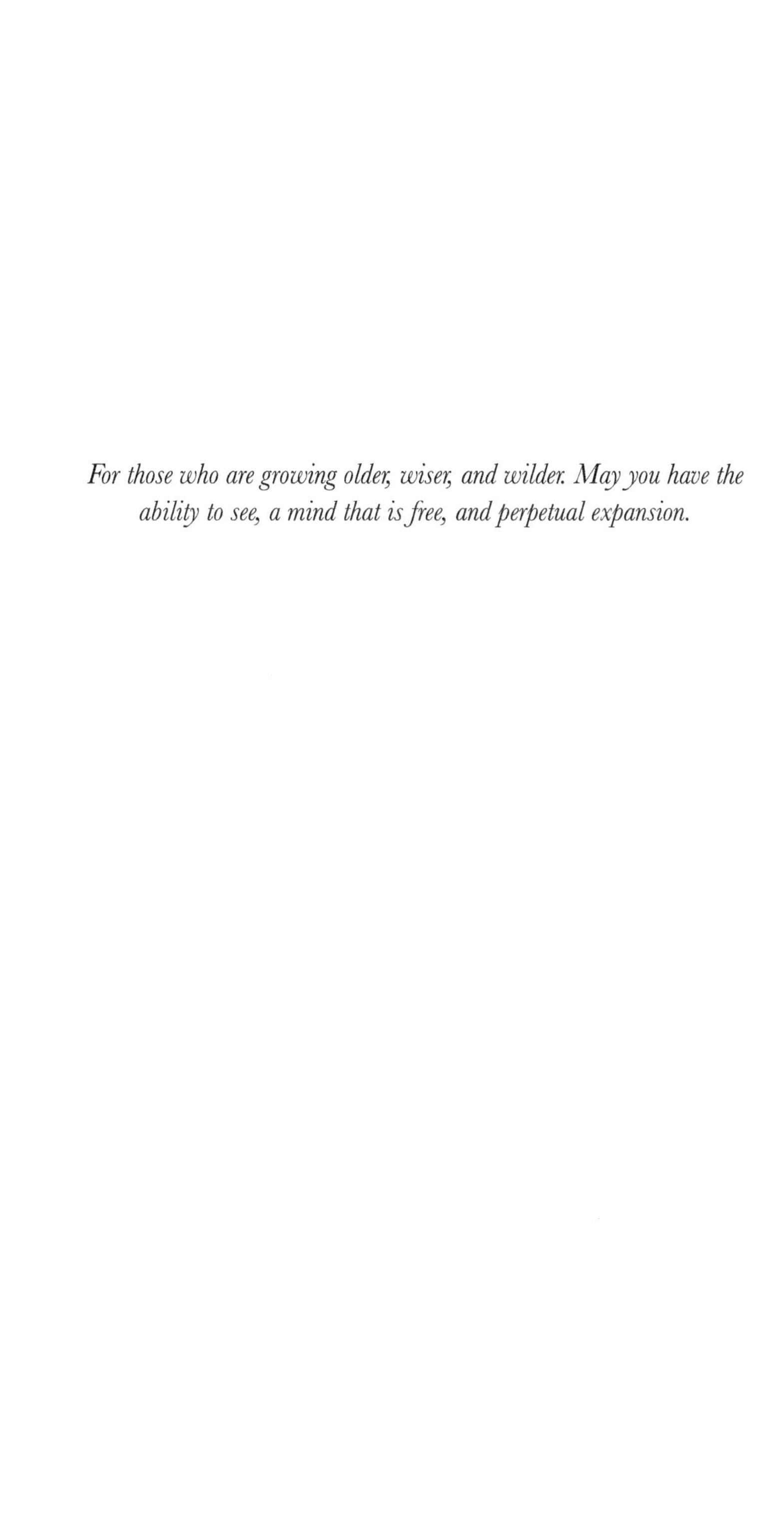

For those who are growing older, wiser, and wilder. May you have the ability to see, a mind that is free, and perpetual expansion.

Contents

Preface

The collection of stories lands on the perfect number: 22. An unplanned magical set, it represents a journey. We matched each piece with a major arcana from the Rider–Waite-Smith (RWS) deck from 0, The Fool, to 21, The World. The Fool represents beginnings, the first step in a long journey to wisdom. None of us are fools, yet many of us have lived with limited access to answers about who we have been and who we can become.

Benebell Wen's **(0 - The Fool) Reclaiming the Witch's Path** presents a starting point, pulling away the cover of hidden histories. In this anthology, we bring together fiction stories embedded with knowledge and essays infused with experience. **(1 - The Magician) Hush** by Lee Murray connects our consciousness to a collective of souls and gathers our tools. Drawing from pain, protection, and power, we speak again. This time with our outside voices.

Human existence requires balance, an interplay of forces and energies. A deep carnal desire to correct history has been brewing in our subconscious. Baigujing is the demoness narrator in Wen Wen Yang's **(2 - The High Priestess)**

Once Upon A Time A Skeleton in the West who shapeshifts into a serpent to bestow violent fates on deserving prey. The archetypal Mother contracts brutality, nurturing our authentic self and balances energies of dark and light. (**3 - The Empress**) **Submission** by Mudang Jenn summons us home to our breath, ignites our curiosities, and tends to our spirits. If Mother supports our spiritual growth then the Father represents authority and structure. In (**4 - The Emperor**) **Beggar's Chicken** by R.F. Whong, the sifu instructs the student to alleviate her own hunger with resourcefulness and grit.

The world has mistreated women, children, the disabled, the neurodivergent, and nonconforming identities. Institutions and organized belief systems have failed these populations with their policies, rules, and processes, gatekeeping resources and dignity. In (**5 - The Hierophant**) **A House That Cannot Fall** by Ai Jiang, the predatory acts of an insurance company and a bank force a widow to call upon her ancestors. Protecting and treating her sick child even when it means her sacrifice is a mother's greatest magic. Glamour spells are driven by love. A practitioner wants others to love her, but she must first love herself. (**6 - The Lovers**) **A Shapeshifter's Hair** by Sam Wilket blends shapeshifter myths from her two cultures and together they empower her modern life. Integrating the past with the present allows us to steer in a desired direction. Dreams are often the realm where worlds meld together. (**7 - The Chariot**) **From the Sea we come, to the Sea we return** by Sobhia Kamal Jamro depicts a cycle in motion, pressing forward while also returning home.

Our life paths require courage, resilience, and inner strength. Poems by M.S. Marquart (**8 - Strength**) **Protection Spells Against Long Covid and ME/CFS** and **When My Long Covid and ME/CFS End Me, Will a**

Mudang be Waiting? capture both the turbulence of life and the joy of living one more day. Mudangs, Shamans, and Priestesses can be advisors and partners. However, the best guide is our intuition, appearing when we most need it. The counsel may appear as a voice or sparks of faulty electricity as it does in **(9 - The Hermit) Hearing Voices** by Angela Yuriko Smith. We only need to allow ourselves to listen and believe.

Our five senses help us commune with the spirits and ancestors. When we cannot see or hear them then smells and tastes don't fail. Passed-down recipes carry sacredness, as in **(10 - Wheel of Fortune) Ingredients Instead** by Ayida Shonibar shows where the secret is the spicy hot fish curry.

With legacy comes accountability, enchantments are not merely fanciful in Frances Lu-Pai Ippolito's **(11 - Justice) Worry Wah Wahs**. The haunted past carries justice to the present. Yet, not every decision is black and white. When judgement suspends, even a meal feels like purgatory. In **(12 - The Hanged Man) We Feed the Hungry Ghost** by T.S. Ren, spirits visit the living in an ever-repeating cycle of unhealed relationships. Family is hard. Regardless of our histories, we long for loved ones after death. In **(13 - Death) Don't Forget Me** by Kristy Park Kulski, patience and rituals for the deceased flow beautifully toward a reunion.

Whether we seek blessings through the light as in **(14 - Temperance) Windows** by Theresa Falk or forge our own faiths in curses like **(15 - The Devil) Rules of Three** by Arushi Karthik, our maternal lines carry the choices forward to future generations. The results are not always immediately apparent. When things fall apart, reconstructing our stories with reverence creates a hopeful future in **(16 - The Tower) Ancestral Worship is Cultural Reinvention** by Pauline Chow highlights destruction as an opportunity to innovate.

Our daily lives are magical. Chaweon Koo breaks down

the most successful magical operation ever executed in **(17 - The Star) Bewitched by K-Pop: High Stakes Ritual Magic for Modern Witches**. Other times, truth hides in nature's quiet rhythm. What messages are found in Gitanjali Lena's poem **(18 - The Moon) My Knees Hurt Like a Village**?

This collection of stories is meant to convince you to believe in our mystical pasts. We have once donned scales like in **(19 - The Sun) The Girl with the Golden Hair** by Sara Surani and **(20 - Judgement) An Ordinary Day in the Life of the White Snake Bai Suzhen as Ms. Lim** by Christine H. Chen. Sonya Rhen's **(21 - The World) Dreams of a Large Oak Tree** articulates the intuition of our dreams, and the possibility of remaking our futures together.

In peace and love,

Angela Yuriko Smith &
Pauline Chow
Co-editors of the Coven of the East

O

Reclaiming the Witch's Path
NONFICTION
Benebell Wen

導江縣有一女巫，人皆肅敬，能逆知人事 …[1]

"There was a witch of the River Dǎo revered by all, who could foretell the affairs of this world …"[2]

The account, be that historical or mythical, comes from the chronicles of a Song dynasty artist and Taoist practitioner.

---

1. From Volume 10 卷十 of Máo Tíng Kè Huà 茅亭客話 [Conversations in the Thatched Pavilion], a collection of cultural commentaries attributed to Huáng Xiūfù 黃休复, a Song dynasty (960 – 1279 AD) Taoist religious painter and calligrapher. Volume 10 recounts the story of a hermit by the name Sun who journeys to Daojiang County (導江縣), in modern-day Sichuan Province, to meet a famous witch 女巫. Note also how "導" (Dǎo) means to lead, direct, and to guide one on a Path, whereas "道" (Dào), as in the Tao, or Taoism, means the Path.
2. Wu 巫 gets translated to witch, but it is the same word as mu 무/巫 for mudang 무당, a Korean shaman, and it is the same word used for the Japanese miko 巫女, a shrine priestess, and note how the Kanji for miko is similar to the characters for a female witch 女巫. Culturally, the wu 巫 is a shaman, and also a priestess who conducts rites and rituals, and also, a witch, depending on how you want to define witch. Thus, "女巫" (nǚwū) is gendered feminine and designates a shaman-priestess, one who performs shamanic witchcraft.

A hermit by the name of Sun journeys to the River Dǎo in search of a renowned witch, acclaimed for her powers and knowledge. He wants to know more about the underworld, about gods, demons, and spirits.

To help answer his questions, the witch channels an ascended master dwelling in the underworld. Now take heed, dear sister, for this thousand-year-old Taoist catechism becomes the cosmological and ethical foundation of the witch's path.

The hermit's first question: "Why do ghosts and spirits harm living people?"

The witch channels the answer: "Ghosts and spirits do not harm living people without reason."

That is to say, there is a cause-and-effect order to the spirit realm. The cosmos is not capricious—a vow was not kept, an act unanswered for, or perhaps an expired bond was not properly severed, and so the unseen will be heard for a reckoning.

The hermit then asks, "Do the gods answer prayers?"

The witch channels the answer, "If one has shown great virtue, and one petitions with sincerity, the gods do bless."

That is an essential insight on spiritual authority, on how gods empower the witch's spell.

The hermit asks a third question. "What is the most serious of transgressions?"

"To end a life in betrayal of one's truth,"[3] answers the witch, channeling the master.

----

3. The original passage reads "殺生與負心爾" (shā shēng yǔ fù xīn ěr). "殺生" (shā shēng) means to kill, to slay, to take away another's life; "負心爾" (fù xīn ěr) means to turn your back on your own heart, to betray one's personal conscience, going against your core values or sense of right and wrong; this is unfaithfulness to oneself and one's own moral compass. The key condition is "與" (yǔ), meaning *and*, a conjunction. To end a life *and* to forsake one's truth, where you shā sheng 殺生 in violation of your own spiritual principles, your xīn 心.

The three questions imply a greater inquiry: How do you live in harmony with both the seen and unseen worlds?

Such is an inquiry of curiosity to the hermit, whereas it holds most weight and impact to the witch, who by nature is an intermediary between the seen and unseen. The two worlds living in harmony is our very purpose. Channeling, divination, mediumship, trance, herbs, talismans, spells, and ritual are our skills.

This parable is a reminder that your spiritual authority as a nǚwū 女巫 comes from walking the path. We practice discernment with every divination, accountability with every rite and ritual, and sincerity with every spell. We seek to understand the motivation of spirits, and we align ourselves with the divinity of gods. Magic is both moral and mystical. To be moral endows the shaman-priestess with divine right; to be mystical is how we cultivate our powers.

For us descendants of the dragon,[4] the story instructs on three key principles of the witch's path:

1. Understand that spirits do not harm without cause. When demons inflict harm, first address what harmed them. The witch's work requires descent into the shadow.
2. When we say that gods answer sincere prayers of the virtuous, we mean that divinity responds to aligned action and intention.
3. To take a life in a manner that severs you from

---

4. "Descendants of the dragon" (龍的傳人, lóong de chuán rén) is a cultural expression that the Han Chinese (Huárén 華人), both those on the native mainland and of the diasporas, use to describe ourselves. We claim ancestry descending from the Yellow Emperor Huangdi 黃帝, who possessed the power to transform himself into a dragon, taught to him by the Lady of the Nine Heavens 九天玄女; hence the ethnonymic epithet "descendants of the dragon."

your own conscience is the gravest transgression of all. That is to say, the most unforgivable act is to slay another in a way that turns you against yourself.

As modern witches inheriting Huáxià 華夏 legacies,[5] we step into a formidable lineage – both historical and mythical – of nǚwū 女巫, shaman-priestesses. May we name and honor the women who embody this parable.

There is Fù Hǎo 婦好, who lived more than three thousand years ago when our gods and ancestors spoke to the shamans through fire-cracked bone and tortoise shell. Fù Hǎo, wife of the Shang dynasty King Wǔdīng 武丁, was a shaman-priestess as well as a military general. She led armies into battle, presided over religious rites, and performed important state divination rituals. Over the millennia, we nǚwū 女巫 venerate Fù Hǎo as one of our ancestral spirits, zǔlíng 祖靈.

During the 4th century Yongjia Massacres, Wèi Huácún 魏華存 escaped the north and brought the Way of the Celestial Masters 天師道 with her to the south. She heard voices, had visions, and the gods spoke through her. These revelations became the sacred Shangqing scriptures of the Way of Supreme Clarity 上清道. Many southern lineages of Taoist mysticism now claim her as their founder. She has been deified as an immortal ascended master to Taoist mystics and priestesses.

There is a Tang dynasty tale about an extraordinary, beautiful girl from the south. A fairy 仙女 appeared to this girl in her visions, revealing the secrets of immortality. Two

---

5. Huáxià 華夏 is a cultural and historical concept dating back to 300 BC, first referenced in the *Zuo Zhuan* 左傳, a seminal Zhou dynasty text on even more ancient Chinese history. "Huáxià" means in the aggregate all Han Chinese people with ancestry traced back to the Yellow River civilizations.

of the Eight Immortals 八仙 taught her mastery over the occult arts.[6] She became Hé Xiāngū 何仙姑, the only identified female among the Eight Immortals. More legendary than historical, Hé Xiāngū is described as a nǚwū 女巫, shaman-priestess, depicted with a white lotus in hand, invoked by modern witches in divination and healing magic. Each year on the eighth night of the eighth new moon, Hé Xiāngū returns to call the next ones forward—the new initiates onto the path. If you invoke her as your patroness and you come sincerely, she will endow you with the gifts of prophecy and healing.

A 10th century maiden from Fujian, Lín Mòniáng 林默娘 was a shaman, a sorceress, a healer. One night a storm pulled a ship under the seas. She rushed out to save the fishermen trapped upon the ship and Lín Mòniáng never returned; instead, from the South Pacific seas emerged the goddess Matsu 媽祖, the deified form of Lín Mòniáng. You'll often find Matsu in temples depicted in triple form 三媽, representing different aspects of her divine persona. She is the goddess called upon by many a spirit medium, the tâng-ki, who channel her. Witches know Matsu not just as a goddess, but as one of us. She inspires us to show up when no one else will, to craft magic from salt, and winds, and sacrifice, always in the name of protecting others.

Also hailing from Fujian is Chén Jìng Gū 陳靖姑 who could commune with spirits. She was a shamanic witch 女巫 with the power to call the rain gods, exorcise demons, perform rituals for abundant harvests, and ensure healthy childbirths. The Taoist mystics of Lúshān 盧山 taught her alchemy, how to craft fu 符 talismans, to banish, to heal, to

---

6. According to lore, the two of the Eight Immortals who were He Xiangu's teachers of magic were Li Tie Guai 李鐵拐, patron divinity of physicians, and the gender-fluid Lan Cai He 藍采和, master of herbalism, weather magic, and a trickster-like figure.

shield. Holy Mother Chén was deeply revered for her compassion and commitment to answering the cries of any who seek her help. Her legacy and deification have transcended regional folklore to be a cultural symbol of social justice magic in advocacy of women.[7]

From 14th century Ming dynasty folklore, Bái Sùzhēn 白素貞 (Madame White Snake) is oft invoked as a patron goddess of witches 女巫. Immortalized in Hangzhou, you can still feel her presence when you walk along the West Lake 西湖. Living some time during the Tang or Song dynasty, she possessed the powers of a snake demon but the heart of a bodhisattva. Madame White Snake could heal as well as she could poison. But men fear what they cannot control. A monk named Fahai, cloaked in righteousness, made it his mission to destroy her. Here is the lesson we learn from Madame White Snake: cultivate strength to defend yourself, but do not let the cruelty of others harden you. Remain gentle in heart and do not betray your good nature. Also, was she a demon? Or is that what we call powerful women who cannot be tamed?

These six immortalized women – witches – transformed history and myth into lineage. They are *our* lineage. This is the coven that connects our ancestral past to you, dear sister,

---

7. In Hokkien folk traditions, the Holy Mother goddess Chén Jìng Gū 陳靖姑 is also presented in triple form, as Holy Mother Chén and two sister assistant goddesses. After the eldest sister Chén, the second sister is Lín Jiǔ Niáng 林九娘. When her family became the target of a malevolent monk's baneful magic, she prayed sincerely to Chén Jìng Gū for help. The goddess taught her defensive magic to defeat the monk. For her heroic act, Sister Lín achieved immortality has a divine emanation of Chén Jìng Gū. The third youngest sister is Lǐ Sān Niáng 李三娘. When she suspected that her good father was being led astray, Sister Lǐ consulted Chén Jìng Gū for clarity and truth. It was then revealed that a sea monster had cast a spell over the good father and the people of the village. Chén Jìng Gū trained Lǐ in Lúshān magic 閭山術法 to defeat the sea monster. Thereafter Sister Lǐ became the third of the triple emanation of Chén Jìng Gū.

in the present day. If the witch of the River Dǎo's parable speaks to you, then you bear the markings of the shaman-priestess. When you reclaim these histories, you restore continuity and awaken your witch powers within.

You've known so little about the magical women of the Hàn 漢 because our foremothers were erased. Those holding the pen on our written histories don't consider these lineages worthy of ink. The legacies of witches and shaman-priestesses, of women psychics, exorcists, spirit mediums, and ghost whisperers are more often than not intentionally forgotten or worse yet, demonized. The history of the shaman-priestess, nüwu 女巫, has in contemporary times become the expelled malevolent crone, wupo 巫婆, deemed a petty old hag who meddles and curses, vilified and re-branded when she became ungovernable, her spiritual authority unverifiable – they tried to strip away her legitimacy by making her grotesque. The vital role of the shaman-priestess waned after Confucian orthodoxy took hold, and make no mistake, the re-branding of the wu 巫 was political.

Yet those few who have resisted erasure, who wielded great power in difficult times, become models for how we can resist being erased ourselves, and how we might channel these zǔlíng 祖靈, our ancestral spirits. When you remember them, their legacies will guide your knowing. These women are your teachers of our ways, of the Dào 道. You reclaiming the witch's path is how we as a coven begin to resist erasure of the nüwu 女巫.

1

Hush

POETRY

Lee Murray

It is an ordinary Tuesday, or possibly a Wednesday, when we hear it, those of us who live. It is morning and also evening, depending on where we have landed, we 巫嫗 witch-sisters from the East. We are willow seedlings dispersed and growing white and spindly in soils beyond the Middle Kingdom, far away from the embrace of the Great Bear. We are a living weave of witch-women, transcending realms and hiding in plain sight. The dead among us, our spirit-mothers, with their ears to the wind and their hearts in the clouds, of course they heard it first, before it was even a whisper, when it was merely a rustle in the trees, a soundless ripple on a silver lake.

Listen, they called. And hush.

in the pot / mother's congee / bubbles

Meanwhile, we, the living witches, are busy with billable hours and research papers, with getting the kids off to school and ourselves to the gym, so we hear it at last, on a Tuesday or possibly a Wednesday, and also at a moment etched in eternity.

It is a girl. It almost always is. She is barely old enough to braid her own hair, though there is nothing wrong with the child's lungs. Her lusty little-girl screams travel across oceans, over deserts and forests, and through heaving cityscapes, to pierce at the heart of us.

She is a fly struggling in a web, while the spider stabs her with its fangs. Not a real spider. That's just a metaphor. More often it is a husband, a father, a brother, or an uncle, but in reality, it is all of them. The perpetrators of the web.

Even as we wonder at the volume emanating from one so tiny, her voice cuts through us with hurt and betrayal. It rips through our quiet complicity, the desperate agony of her cries seizing at our insides, seething and simmering in our bones. It is not the first time. It is not even the millionth time. We have endured worse, we tell ourselves.

the radio blares / a song played on repeat

Only, her shrieks go on and on and on.

Hush now. We work our enchantment over her, will her to be quiet. But she is frantic. Frightened. It is an old story, one where men have the upper hand. Occasionally, the plot may vary although the theme has remained the same: when there is not enough, or even when there is, a girl must give in or go without. She is to be devoured, deflowered, denied. It is the way it is, the way it has always been.

We remember the tale about the girl murdered so some dead sap might have a wife to look after him in the afterlife. The one about the girl slaughtered like a pig, sliced and salted, so her family might eat. The one where the daughter-in-law worked herself to the bone to support her good-for-nothing husband. The one where the girl is forced against her will. Where she gave up her dreams …

Remember all the girl babies they made us smother.

That doesn't happen anymore. Does it?

Does it?

millet droops / under a blazing sun

The child is keening so loudly that she cannot not hear us bickering. To be fair, we can scarcely hear ourselves over the din. We cringe and chafe at her discomfort. Some of us know her agony. The others can relate. It is common enough.

Keep her quiet, hiss the dead.

She is so young, we tell our departed sisters, our mothers, our aunties. Too young, we tell ourselves. How could she know? There hasn't been time to teach her all the rules.

Nevertheless, the aunties insist she must be silenced. For all our sakes.

So we urge her to be quiet, the force of our collective magic focused on dampening her wailing. Hush now, little one. Hush, hush. It's for the greater good. A small sacrifice to keep us all safe. Little steps, small breaths. It is best if we are small and deathly quiet, like Mao's sparrows. They must not hear us. Let go of want. Forget yourself. It will be over soon.

Still, the child bucks and shrieks beneath her oppressor. She's a feisty one, no doubt about it. We witch sisters shake our heads in despair. Lost to pain and fear, the child doesn't understand. We wish it were quicker – it's easier when it is quick – but sometimes these things go on for years. Poor little thing. We have seen it before.

there it is / that song again

Noooo! Stop! Please.

We wish he would stop because it is all we can do, we witch sisters in our cosmic coven, to hold back the girl's cavernous, cacophonous pain. Just one child yet from her flows an ocean of trauma and injustice. It rolls over us in relentless waves.

Wave after wave after wave.

Naturally, we witch sisters do what we always have. We hold back the surge, hold ground, even in these faraway foreign realms. We plant our feet and gather in the noise, catching it up in our own quiet net of complicity. Absorbing it into ourselves until we are swollen with hate and hurt and pain. We swallow the noise.

Swallow it down.

Submit, subsume, subjugate.

Hush, girl.

Hush, hush.

Swallow it down.

This little one is not like the others. Or perhaps she is exactly like the others, but strangely, it seems the moment has changed. This Tuesday or possibly a Wednesday, something feels different. Something pivotal and poignant.

Today, the air is redolent with hunger and want.

I won't, the girl yells – and we gasp.

Shocked, some of us drop the spell. The sound rolls in.

The dead ones don't miss a trick; they snatch up the cries and funnel them away. No, no, no. Don't listen, don't listen, the old ones rail. We must keep the girl quiet, hold back her clamour. It's for the best. It's for the good of us all. We must stay out of sight, beyond their hearing, beneath their notice. That has always been our power.

rocks / tumbling / on the riverbed

Our power?

We are many, says an academic among us. Look at our collective strength. Between us, we have muffled the screams for centuries.

Another, a lawyer, speaks of other kinds of enchantments. Of procedures and proceedings. Of protections.

Wait? We could undo the spell? Break the web?

We are many, the researcher reminds us.

The dead, our mothers and our aunties, clamour against it. But this is the only way we know, they say. It is the way it is, the way it has always been. For generations, we have maintained the hush to keep our daughters safe.

Except we are not safe, those of us who live protest. See this little girl. Hear her screams. There is no safety in submission. No safety in silence. Only pursed lips and purgatory, rising rage and resentment.

It's just one girl, insist the dead. One girl.

It is all girls, we counter.

We've endured worse, our spirit-mothers wail. And now you will reject us, disregard our teachings, throw over tradition. It will be as if we never lived.

No, no, we answer. We will never forget you, our spirit-mothers. You did your best to keep us safe, it is true. We are grateful for your sacrifice. But something has changed. All at once we are a weave of 巫嫗 witch-women, sisters transcending realms, who are no longer content to hide in plain sight. Today begins a new era, and for that we need a new spell. We must sing a new song, dredge it up from deep in our bones, and project it from our lungs, so that even the Great Bear will hear us from the heavens.

The living blink in awe. The dead among us pause.

The coven takes a collective breath, and we straighten. It is decided then. So it is an ordinary Tuesday, and in some places a Wednesday, but nevertheless it is an auspicious day, when we let the net fall and step aside, when we let the wave crash where it will.

No, we will not hush.

We will not be hushed.

All around us, the noise swells.

late summer / the mosquitoes swarm

2

Once Upon a Time a Skeleton in the West

FICTION

Wen Wen Yang

I will grant you that Sun Wukong bested me in China, but he did not kill me. Weakened, I went to the shore to recover. Ships brought new men every day. Perhaps one of them was a holy monk whose flesh could bestow immortality. Instead, I saw dozens of girls, chained, boarding a ship. The girl at the very end broke free from the chains, the cuffs scraping her skin as she wiggled free. She ran, disappearing into the crowd. I stared at the swinging manacles.

My injuries still stung, my flesh soft as an overripe peach. I had been left for dead, why not go on an adventure? I transformed into a young girl and joined the group, slipping my slender wrists through the metal.

Onboard the tossing ship, the girls exchanged stories. They had been sold for $50 apiece. I borrowed the hollow cheeks and bellies of one girl's family. I had seen enough suffering in my time that the lies came easily. They listened with horror that my mother's hair fell out as well. Their eyes grew wet, imagining my father struggling to chew with his remaining teeth. Of course they had sold me.

On the journey, girls cried and died. Older girls took

turns comforting the younger ones. I was a skeleton under my human disguise. Of course I survived, no matter how putrid the food, how foul the water.

At the dock, men separated the girls. I considered shifting my face to appear more beautiful, smooth skin and large eyes, but the men were laughing. The beautiful would become concubines in gilded cages. Once their beauty waned or if they failed to please their masters, they would return to the auction block. Sold like cattle or a well used wagon.

The girl beside me had bound feet. "They'll pay fifty cents just to touch her feet!" The men jeered. She was sold for $200.

I stayed plain, hiding my white lotus face.

Six ghosts, also young girls, saw through my disguise. They howled in my twitching ears. *Báigǔjīng*, they whispered, *kill them all!* They had eaten raw opium, how they still stank of it!

Leering patrons walked through the ghosts as if they were dust. Coins jingled in their pockets, a threat that they could afford a piece of us. As if their stares were knives, I could feel their stare cut into my chest down to my knees. Some of the men wore badges, polished to shine in the sunlight. No wonder these girls ran and welcomed death.

I wanted to taste their flesh. What did it feel like to not fear an attack from a predator? Did it make them unable to detect danger, never looking over their shoulder for something smaller, until it was close enough to bite? Perhaps they saw me like a flea, easily crushed between their nails.

The city was close enough to the wilderness, wooden sidewalks rotting into the desert sand. The smell of human civilization, their sweat and garbage, and the waste of their animals: cows, horses, dogs. The dogs snapped at me, trusting their noses over their eyes.

When I followed the man who bought me, I felt the stares. The sailors, teenage boys, drunks and day laborers, all ready to break my spirit for twenty-five cents, fifty cents at a time.

My bloodlust still pulsed through me. Which would taste the best? The man snoozing in front of the saloon, or the wiry muscled man on a horse, giant hat hiding his face in shadow?

The other dead girls gathered in welcome. Some had caught incurable diseases. Their nails and fingers were broken from trying to escape windowless cells where they starved to death. Some girls' hair dripped sea water, having jumped into the ocean that separated us from home. Did they plan to swim home, or did they fill their pockets with rocks first?

The women in the brothel saw us coming, their faces disappearing behind barred windows.

The ghosts followed me into the brothel, past impressive doors that locked women in. The brothel owner was stout, skin pitted like orange skin. A queue hung down his back like any other Chinese man outside. A gun was holstered on his hip.

The ghosts snarled at him, but they had never learned how to harness chi. He didn't seem to notice their ghostly hands trying to strike his throat or grasp his heart. I smelled his breakfast on his breath, mixed with tobacco. I stared defiantly, willing him to see the danger in my eyes.

"Are you going to be obedient?" he barked.

"No," I started. The syllable felt like a new fang in my mouth.

He backhanded me across the face.

The pain bloomed, blinding me to the second blow.

"Are you going to be a troublemaker?"

The skin stripped from my face, revealing my skeletal

form. Claws, fangs and a tail. I was well rested from the journey, devouring girls who died overnight before the crew could throw them overboard. They always assumed the girl had jumped into the ocean. Their flesh had been so soft, so sweet.

He unholstered his gun.

I grinned. "Death will not take me." I dissolved into my true form, a pile of flour white bones. They rattled apart.

Bang, bang, bang.

"What demon is this?" he cried, teeth clenched and spittle flying.

Bang, bang, bang. His bullets rang wild, through his furniture, windows and walls, instead of bone.

When his gun clicked empty, he started to shout for help. I reformed my jade bones, folding flesh overtop.

I launched myself at his neck. My claws opened his jugular, his blood warming my ice-white skin. He tried to scream but the blood choked his words. The fountain spurting from his neck lessened to a gurgling leak.

His death rattle was barely above a whimper. An ever widening pool of blood stained the floor, stained my white gauze skirt.

"A ghost," a woman gasped as she entered the room. "A devil!" She bowed, pressing her forehead nearly to my feet. His blood stained her hands, outlined her fingers. "Thank you, thank you."

As I licked my fingers clean, the ghosts' whispered for their own revenge.

My owner still has my daughter.

I don't know where they sold my sister.

There was no shortage of deserving men here, no shortage of prey. Yes, I would have an adventure, indeed!

Submission
FICTION

Mudang Jenn

Sometimes it starts with a little tickle. Then comes a whisper from within. The call to explore your spirituality, connect with your spirits, or something greater. It's your soul stirring, your spirit speaking, your ancestors stepping forth. The drums will call for you, igniting something within. A part of you has awakened and listens. The return begins, a journey back to yourself, to your spirits, a journey back home.

THE UNFURLING OF YOUR PRACTICE, your sacred rituals is the journey of getting to know your own inner spirits. Coming home to you, yourself, your breath. You must connect with yourself. It is the root, the foundation, from which all will grow. Before meeting with the spirits, you must meet with yourself.

When I first walked this path as a Korean shaman, known as a mudang, one of the first teachings I received was the importance of the vessel, our body. Like a potter shaping clay and forging a vessel meant to hold something sacred. We are the vessel that carries the waters of spirit … our own, our ancestors and those yet to come. But as we begin this journey many of us in the diaspora carry uncertainty. We carry grief, pressure and questions no one prepared us for.

Before I ever stepped into ceremony or picked up a drum, I remembered that our power as mudangs comes from what was passed down. Not by ritual but through blood, breath and story.

Mythology and stories shape how we understand society, power, and roles. In Korea, many of the stories have been filtered through a Confucian lens that elevates men while silencing women. The myth of Dangun, god king of Korea, is a celebrated origin story of royal masculine authority. Yet if you look closer, another story is hidden within it, the story of his mother, the first mudang, Ungnyeo the Bear.

Ungnyeo mythology reveals a deeper spiritual power of the women, the feminine and matriarchs within our family and societies. If Dangun's story is Korea's origin myth, then Ungnyeo's story may be the origin myth of the first mudang.

Ungnyeo entered a cave to transform from bear to human only consuming sacred herbs of garlic and mugwort. After 21 days, Ungnyeo was no longer a bear but transformed into a human of sacred power. Desiring a child, she went to a sacred birch tree and prayed to the Heavens. Her prayers moved Hwanung, the son of Hwanin, the ruler of the skies. Hwanung descended, fulfilling Ungnyeo's prayer and ritual. Later Ungnyeo gave birth to Dangun, the god king of Korea.

This is the myth of transformation. Of ritual, prayer and devotion.

It speaks to the hidden feminine power that runs through our stories. The stories of the ignored, the forgotten and rewritten. The bear is more than just a symbol, she is the mother of people birthed through ritual and prayer, the ancestor to all mudangs. The ancestor to feminine power, and represent the power within our matriarchs and lineages. In Ungnyeo's story we are given tools for reclaiming matriarchal and embodied wisdom. Wisdom that lives within our lineages, our bodies and our breath.

In the early stages of our return to our spiritual practice there can be a ripple of panic. Fear of getting it wrong. A deep ache to belong to something we were once cut off from. And so, we try to earn our place. We follow instructions and we mimic the motions. We confuse discipline for devotion. Rigid practice without deeper meaning creates cracks in the vessel. Instead of holding spirit, we begin to leak energy. Real medicine doesn't come from perfect steps. It's made from relationships. How present you are in the rituals, the sincerity of your breath, the feeling behind your offerings, the connection you're cultivating when you show up.

This is the heart of the practice.

Being in relationship with spirit, with your people, with yourself, with the land you walk on.

Ritual isn't a checklist. It's the expression of your soul. You don't need more intricate steps, you need meaning. And when spoken with sincerity, your simple acts of ritual will become sacred.

Drums are an important instrument in rituals and ceremonies for mudangs. The beat and vibration of the drum is meant to ring the heavens and awaken the earth, calling out to it and commanding attention. Our body, the vessel, is that drum.

In ceremony we pay close attention to how our bodies are feeling, we turn inward focusing below the surface, of what may be buried or remains unseen.

This is how we come into ceremony with our body, our drum. Let your body guide you. Tap your chest lightly and gently let the rhythm arise from within. Depending on the song that arises, let your body lead you, telling you what it needs. Allow your body to unfurl, to release, to breath.

In joy and celebrations, we say our shoulders become light, they bounce around with laughter. Watching elderly Korean grandmothers when they dance, shoulders swaying and their arms lifted up in the air. Joy rippling through their bodies. But when we carry pain, silence and grief our shoulders become heavy, burdened by what we carry, by what we hold without release. In Korean shamanic kut ceremonies, we carefully watch the body as it reveals what spirits are carrying.

We can call this heavy weight, *han*. Rather than having a rigid definition, han is felt. It's poetic, raw and deeply human. It lives in silence, in what remains unseen. Lingers in the unsaid. And it begins to release slowly only when given space to be expressed.

These practices aren't meant to escape the world.

They are how we return to it, more present, rooted and human.

We practice so that we may move through it with presence and purpose.

Spirits don't need or want your perfection. They need your presence.

4

Beggar's Chicken

HYBRID

R. F. Whong

Wang Jun opened her eyes. Her body ached, and her stomach growled.

The afternoon sunlight filtered through the canopy, casting dappled patterns on the ground. She left the cavern. Under the warming sun rays, the injuries on her flesh appeared skin-deep, nothing to worry about. A patch of bright yellow fruits off to her left caught her attention. She examined them to ensure they were indeed wild loquat, then plucked a handful. The sweet, slightly tart flavor provided momentary relief from her hunger.

After eating more loquats but still not sated, she mumbled under her breath, "Are there wild chickens in the region?"

Images of yesterday's shipwreck arose unbidden in her mind. Where were Sifu and the others? Was she the sole soul cast adrift upon this isolated isle? She lowered her gaze and pondered a lesson her sifu had imparted.

"In Southern China," Sifu Chun had taught her, "the red jungle fowl roam free. Their call is distinct—a rhythmic cadence that can guide you when food is scarce."

Jun's lips crinkled up. She turned her ears to the symphony of forest sounds. Her heart quickened as a distinctive call reached her. The recollection surged forth with vivid clarity. Sifu had instructed her every day in the art of hurling a chopstick or a rock toward sundry targets.

Her smile widened. She picked up three small rocks and proceeded through the underbrush, every muffled step a reflection of knowledge she learned from Sifu. A silhouette with vibrant hues came into view. She hurled a rock. It grazed and startled the bird. The fowl took off. Adjusting her aim in haste, she launched a second one. This time, it struck the target in midair with fatal precision.

Jun gathered moist clay from a stream bank to encase the whole bird, then dug a pit in the earth. Striking a flint-like stone against the iron pin on her rowboat's oar, she coaxed a shower of sparks and directed them toward a bundle of dried grasses. As a few stubborn sparks settled into the tinder, she fed it brittle twigs. When the flame blazed, she dropped the clay-encased bird into the center of the pit and piled on more branches and deadwood.

A pleasant aroma permeated the air, each wisp a delicious taunt to her insistent hunger. At last, she retrieved her preparation and cracked open the hardened mound of mud. The outer shell peeled away together with the feathers to reveal the tender fowl.

WHAT WOULD you do if you were a kung fu master and landed on a remote island without food?

In the above story, as Wang Jun explored the dense, tropical landscape, she used her skill to catch a fowl. Without cooking utensils, she followed a well-known Chinese recipe called "The Beggar's Chicken" to cook her bird.

Beggar's Chicken, a dish originating from eastern China, is a gastronomic delight steeped in tradition, ingenuity, and timeless culinary flair. This beloved dish exemplifies not only the ability to create delicious food using simple ingredients but also the profound relationship between culture and cuisine.

The legend of Beggar's Chicken is as enchanting as the dish itself. As the story goes, a destitute beggar in imperial China stumbled upon a chicken, but lacking any cooking utensils, was forced to come up with an ingenious solution. He coated the whole chicken (uncleaned, ungutted, with feathers) in mud and placed it in a makeshift fire pit to bake. When he cracked open the hardened mud shell and peeled it away together with the feathers, a tender and aromatic chicken awaited inside. The delightful aroma attracted the attention of passing royal members, who were so impressed that the dish was adopted and refined in the imperial kitchen.

At the heart of Beggar's Chicken is a whole chicken encased in a layer of clay before being roasted. Later versions use a cleaned, gutted chicken stuffed with spices such as ginger, star anise, soy sauce, Shaoxing wine, and garlic. The preparation of Beggar's Chicken requires patience to encase the bird meticulously and wait for the slow cooking process to work its magic.

Beggar's Chicken is a reminder of the ingenuity rooted in Chinese cuisine, where simplicity meets sophistication. It highlights the importance of resourcefulness and the ability to elevate basic ingredients to something flavorful and memorable. The story behind the dish also touches on themes of transformation and creativity, rendering it a cultural emblem that resonates well beyond its taste.

Modern renditions of Beggar's Chicken may not involve mud encasements, but chefs often use a bread dough wrap or stick with a less traditional approach using foil or parchment paper. Despite these adaptations, the essence of the dish remains as an homage to an ingenious story, allowing the chicken to be steamed within its own juices to concentrate its essence.

Eating Beggar's Chicken is more of an event than a mere meal. The cracking open of the hardened layer brings an element of drama. The tender meat, easily coming off the bone, is a testament to its thoughtful preparation.

5

A House That Cannot Fall
FICTION

Ai Jiang

The first thought I have when I enter the lobby of the life insurance company at 3 p.m. is how many people have already arrived and gone with the ghosts of their loved ones tethered to their shadows.

"I ... am here to claim my husband's life insurance," I say, and these aren't words I ever thought I would utter in this lifetime.

The receptionist looks at me, at my ID, pauses, then taps at her keyboard, stares at the screen then back at me. "We'll need your husband to sign off on it."

"Sign off ... on his own life insurance ...?" My fingers paw at the empty space where my pawned wedding ring used to sit, specifically because I'd heard horrors like these, feared they would come to fruition.

"Yes." The receptionist doesn't bother looking up and refocuses on her computer.

"But—" I slowly slide my ID off the desk. Why did she even ask me for it then, if she knew she couldn't help me? "He's dead."

"Yes, but we still need his signature."

"Do you not understand what I'm saying?" My hand twitches where it rests on my bag with the sudden urge to grab the receptionist's collar though I know there's nothing she can do about the rules set in front of her, even if they make no sense.

Her expression is one of pity as she sighs, heavy and long, but underlying is a growing impatience as she clicks her nails against the receiver of the phone next to her, probably wondering if she should call security. "Yes, I understand, but we still—"

I turn and walk out of the lobby.

The bank says the exact same thing. I have the exact same conversation with them, and it ends the exact same way. For all the widows. Every time. I should've known.

I leave without having accomplished anything, because you're waiting for me at home, but it's a home that we might be soon losing.

Even when I return the next day and the next, the life insurance company says the same thing, and so does the bank, and I wonder which of us might be worn down first, and I can already tell it is me, but I can't bring back to life someone whose body has already cooled, no matter how much I want to.

YOU'VE BEEN sick for longer than you've ever been, but the doctor can't figure out why.

Your medicine is on the highest shelf in the kitchen because I know you love to climb counters when I'm not at home even though your chin just brushes the surface of the dining table. I'm balancing precariously on a stool as you watch from below. But when my hand wraps around the medicine bottle, it's empty.

My free hand trembles against the shelf door, nails scratching against the peeling paint. That is when your bellows begin from behind—an eagle's cry from your human lips. Squawks that quickly become wails, then increase in pitch and volume until they become shrieks. I almost topple off the stool when I let go of the shelf door and drop the bottle to cover my ears.

I stumble off, my feet almost slipping when they meet the ceramic of the kitchen tiles, towards you. I pull you to me, whispering, "It's okay, it's okay, it's okay," even though my lungs are searing, lips cracked and dry, skull splitting from your voice now ringing—far too loud.

"I understand," I say.

"It hurts. It hurts. It does. It does. Make it stop," you say. "Everything. Everything."

I lay a hand on the top of your head, wrap my fingers over your fist clenched against your chest. Pills cannot fix you —only numb the pain, temporarily.

So instead, I slide the jade bangle my mother gave me off my wrist with the help of vegetable oil. It's heavy and cold in my hands, a swirl of emerald, pale green, and white like dispersing ink in water. Grandmother, my mother, and all my aunties, said that wearing jade will protect us from danger, that when we're on the verge of death the jade will break in two, shatter into small pieces, but its wearer will stay whole, alive.

I slip the jade bracelet around your wrist, but I don't know if it's something that can save you from yourself.

ON THE WAY to Mother's shrine, there are potholes, cracks in the concrete, weeds growing on sidewalks that melt into fields and dirt roads. The former two can't be good omens.

When I light incense for Mother at her altar, I ask, "Why is she not recovering?" as I wait for her spirit to appear, but she often takes her time, even when I don't have any to spare.

Then, finally, she emerges as a wisp along with the smoke of the incense—her voice, pitched, hollow yet not, like the trickle of a small stream over pebbles and palm-sized mountains with peaks of moss and algae rather than snow, smoothed out jagged slate rather than ever-changing terrain, echoes my name.

"Because you chew for her, you speak for her, you fall for her," Mother says. "Child, if I do that for you, if you do that for your own child, then how can you, how can she, ever hope to survive on her own when you are gone?"

"When I'm gone …"

"Yes, when you're gone."

"I will build her a home that will never fall."

"And how will you do that?" Mother's remaining eye blazes with such a ferocity it almost burns to stare for too long, like a flaming star approaching, its surface boiling, and the searing liquid threatening to spill and splash my way.

As if she already knows the answer, she waits.

"The way you have done for me."

WITHOUT YOUR FATHER, the mortgage and bills must still be paid somehow, and the house still needs renovations. If I can't pay for it in cash, I will have to pay for it with my life essence, with my flesh and bone, and hope that will be enough.

I bottle up parts of my soul and peddle it at the black market, and for you, as you grow, I pull strands of my hair, lay them out on the table, and thread them through the bone of my pinky, severed and carved into several fine needles. I sharpen the gutting knife, sterilize it, before holding it up to my collarbone. By the end of the week, the house is mended, every inch patched, and you have fine new clothing, dolls, and your hunger finally sated, your pain finally waned.

I lie down and gasp every time I move because the air kisses my open wounds and refuses to let go. Then I still, even when you come to sit next to me during my last breaths.

A house is only as good as how it's been cared for, a child only as strong as the armor she's equipped with, was something Mother always told me.

Have I done enough to equip you?

There is a glimmer of sunrise held in your eyes—a startling, hopeful contrast to the bleeding sunset I've become—as you pull my skin taut against your small frame, rocking your bare feet back and forth, back and forth against the floor now also made of me, nestled in a home that cannot fall.

This is more than I could've asked for—the best view at the end of the road: you.

6

A Shapeshifter's Hair
NONFICTION
Sam Wilket

My mother's magic was glamour. When I was small, I would sit outside the open bathroom door and watch as she performed her morning ritual at the altar of our fluorescent-lit mirror. She worked layers of buttery foundation into her face and neck, leaving her skin smooth as a pearl and nearly as light. When she emerged, she was a different person: polished, professional, pale. She was certainly still Chinese, but something fundamental about her had changed. Once she slipped into a sleek skirt suit and tucked away every trace of her accent, she looked like she could walk into any office and belong there. My mother never said she didn't want to be Chinese, but I absorbed the message nonetheless.

The men she dated were another clue. My father was white and, after they got divorced, all her boyfriends were too. I don't remember her ever calling a Chinese person beautiful. Looking back, I see that many of the things my mother praised me for were badges of my whiteness. She fawned over my freckles and my height. She was short, only five foot one, and by the time I was a preteen I towered over her. She glowed as she wrapped her arm around my waist and boasted to her friends that I was still growing.

Most of all she adored my hair, which is dark but lighter than hers, with hints of red from my British father's side. When I was young, my mom insisted I keep it long, at least halfway down my back. Before I went to my dad's on weekends, she would weave my hair into two French braids and order him not to touch it. I returned to her with the braids sleep-mussed and greasy, but otherwise intact. As I got older, I learned there is shapeshifting magic in my mixed-race hair. When I wear it loose, framing my pale, freckled face, I walk through the world as a white woman. When I tie my hair back, I become something else entirely: an exotic, unclassifiable creature. Most of my life, I've felt more comfortable with my hair down. Only recently have I started to ask myself, why?

IN MYTHS from my British lineage, witches were believed to have shapeshifting powers. Many tales tell of witches transforming into cats or hares. In a story from the 1700s, a man is kept awake for several nights by yowling cats, which he becomes convinced are witches in disguise. One night, exhausted and raging, he rushes out of his house and attacks the cats with a hatchet, killing two and wounding several others. The next day, two local women are found to have suddenly died overnight, and another has a hatchet wound in her leg so deep that she will lose the limb.

WHEN I WAS AROUND THIRTEEN, I finally convinced my mother to let me cut my hair. I was obsessed with the X-Files at the time, and especially its main female character: brilliant, beautiful FBI Agent Dana Scully. I admired everything about her, including the way her signature auburn bob framed her delicate, porcelain face. Even as I cut the photo out of the magazine, I knew I looked nothing like her. My face was rounder, my nose wider, my ears larger. My hair was dark and coarse, and frizzed at the slightest suggestion of humidity. Over the summer, my legs sprouted up and my hips stretched out. The XXL t-shirts I was hiding in weren't fooling anyone into thinking I was petite. Still, I handed the hairdresser the photograph.

With the first cut, the right side of my hair was severed above my shoulder. The newly short ends bounced and flipped out at odd angles. I started to cry. I watched in the mirror as the other side was chopped off, staring at the stranger in the glass with flecks of dark hair stuck to her bare neck, tears glistening on her cheeks, her mouth set in a grim line. My mother looked on from behind me, disappointment creasing her carefully painted face.

In the months that followed I felt more monstrous than ever, exposed without the curtain of my hair to shield me. My brittle illusion of belonging shattered, as questions I had previously brushed off now came in stinging waves too frequent to dodge. *What are you? Where are you from?* Each one left me off-balance and wounded, more vulnerable to the next blow, until my hair grew back and returned me to my other form.

IN FOLKTALES from my Chinese lineage, fox spirits often take the form of beautiful, clever, and sometimes lustful women. In many of these stories, fox spirits are eager to shake off their supernatural identities and become passionate lovers or caring wives to mortal men. In one famous story, a fox spirit takes the form of a gorgeous woman named Miss Ren and a man named Zheng falls in love with her. They start a life together, Miss Ren remaining all the while in her human form. But one day, as Miss Ren and Zheng travel between two towns, they encounter a party of hunters. The hunters' dogs try to attack Miss Ren and she flees, transforming into her fox spirit form in an attempt to escape. But she isn't fast enough. The dogs chase her down and kill her. No matter how long Miss Ren lived as a human, her fox form remained a part of her. Denying it led to her downfall.

IN MY EARLY THIRTIES, I was working for a tech company whose office was a half hour commute from my apartment. Running late one morning, I swept my hair into a bun and burst out my front door, sprinting for the bus. I reached my desk with a couple minutes to spare and melted into my chair with relief.

"Excuse me—"

A colleague loomed over me, awkwardly smoothing a hand over his dark beard. He sat a couple desks over, a software developer. He'd taught me how to use the fancy company espresso machine on my first day, four years ago, and we'd exchanged collegial waves every morning since.

"Oh!" I pushed a strand of hair behind my ear, as cover for wiping the sweat off my forehead. "Hi."

His eyes flicked over my bare desk.

"Are you new here? You need to check in at the front."

"What?" I said. "It's me."

He frowned, then his eyes widened. "I'm so sorry! I didn't recognize you. Your hair—" he laughed, but his smile carried a current of accusation underneath. "It's so cool that you can completely transform, just by putting your hair up."

My instinct was to bow my head and let my hair obscure my flaming cheeks, but every strand was slicked back, pulled tightly to my skull. There was nothing to hide behind. Then something in me shifted. I realized he was seeing me, not in one guise or another, but in my true form: a shapeshifter, a being with the power to choose what shape to appear in, and when. How did I not see it as *power*, before? But I could see it now, and I knew it was mine to claim. I swallowed, pushed my shoulders back, and looked him right in the eye.

"Yes," I said, giving him a smile that showed my teeth. "It is."

7

From the Sea We Come, to the Sea We Return

FICTION

Sobhia Kamal Jamro

Suhni came to me in a dream. A dream about drowning. All I remember is a huge flood coming over Karachi from the south, from the Sea that my people have fished for centuries, millennia. The fishermen went first, their lifeless bodies floating in the same water as their straw huts and mud from the land they called home. The water that was coming to devour me too. My heart lurched and fear crept up my throat. But my feet remained planted on the ground. I could not run. I knew it was revenge. Either the fishermen's or God's. If these were older times, before Islam and monotheism, there would be no difference between the two. The Sustainer, God is called. The fishermen sustained people all over Karachi and Pakistan. But then cities and factories were built, and all the waste was dumped into the Sea, endangering sea-life. The fishermen then struggled to sustain their own families. The Sea was getting angrier by the day and the fishermen could tell. When they sailed, they could feel the waves growling under their patched up boats. They trembled in fear, but if they let fear win, they would starve. So they carried their fishing on, satisfied with what little they could find in the polluted water. But now the Sea had finally attacked. No, not attacked. Defended. I closed my eyes and took a long, last breath.

When the enormous wave came, it first slammed me into the ground. Quiet chaos. Then, I was hauled up from the ground and thrown around by the water like a ragdoll. Then, I floated. The water calmed quickly and there was silence. I tried opening my eyes but the sand in the water rubbed against them, almost blinding me. My lungs were burning. I couldn't even see my own hands. I could only vaguely sense where my body was. My head was simultaneously heavy and light and suddenly I remembered that I was in a dream. I could simply decide to live. I took a deep breath in. And then another. And another. No water went into my lungs and no air. But I was alive. I kept breathing.

From my right, I felt a rush of water wash over me and move past. The rest was disturbed. Seconds later, a stronger rush. The waves were slowly moving clockwise. I was being elevated—simultaneously pushed upwards and sideways, in a spiral. No ... a tornado? In the middle of the city? The waves grew more violent, acting with a mind of their own. I felt like I was in the rumbling belly of a monster. I was being moved too fast, the blood in my head rushing. Once or twice something brushed past me, almost injuring me. The rush of the waves was deafening. My intuition told me the tornado was retreating, going back the direction it came from, into the Sea. I crouched, pushing my head between my knees and wrapping my arms around them. As long as nothing hit my head or heart, I was safe. Just then, something large and hard slammed against my body from the right. The force broke my protective formation and turned me sideways. Another hard thing slammed into me, something that felt like a human body. My heart had been hit. The pain made it harder to crouch again but I managed. The pain made my head spin faster. I was awake one moment and asleep in another.

The tornado was moving fast. When it arrived at the Sea, the momentum broke and I was slowly lowered into the surface of the water. When my body touched the sea water, I shivered. The water was cold. Slowly, I sank. I could open my eyes now. The water was clearer, and I could see fish swimming by, all kinds of fish. I wanted to go deeper, deeper. I have always wondered what lay further in the Sea than where humans can go.

I swam for hours until far in the distance, somewhere on the sea-bed, I saw a fire burning. A red and orange fire. I thought of Moses and went towards it. Were we wrong about God and Heaven being above us? Was it in the depths of the Sea all along? But why would someone like me be invited to see God? My body moved mechanically. My arms pushed water out of the way and my feet paddled on their own. The closer I moved to the fire, the bigger it grew.

The fire was burning on firewood, as a traditional camp-fire would, with logs leaning vertically on each other, like a tent. The seascape revealed itself to me slowly, like a magic spell being lifted off. A small house appeared, made of wood, with a veranda and large windows. Around the house, seaweed grew and fish swam idly by, but the house and the fire remained standing on solid ground. When I drew closer to the house, I saw a beautiful woman with deep, walnut brown hair that flowed down her waist—the most beautiful woman I had ever seen. She was wearing a soft maroon choli and lehenga, embroidered in golden thread. She beamed when she saw me. Behind her the cottage door opened and out came a beautiful man. A tall man with dark black hair and a mustache, a light beard and skin tanned from long hours under the sun. He smiled at me too. I willed myself to learn the identity of these two people. I should know, this was my dream.

The woman was Suhni and the man was Mehar, the two lovers from the folktale told to me over and over again since I was a child. Suhni drowned in River Indus and Mehar, distraught, jumped in after her. Could it be that the river had led them to the Sea?

"So this is what became of you?" I said to Suhni, and then, looking at the man behind her, "And Mehar? How did he find you? Or you him?" She said nothing but walked towards me, like a dancer and a queen, someone with both power and control. I suddenly felt afraid.

"Did you cause the flood?" I asked more solemnly. I didn't want it to be her. Mehar stood leaned against the door of the cottage behind her. Suhni was now before me and raised her hands. I recoiled and stepped away.

"Don't be afraid," she said, her voice echoing through the vast nothingness in the water, sending shivers down my back. But her words worked like a spell—all fear left my body. She stepped towards me again and held my face in both her hands. "Don't be afraid," she said more softly now, more human, "Come inside, you've travelled long. Sleep here tonight. We will look after you."

Suddenly sleep washed over my whole body, my eyelids became heavier every passing moment. I nodded my head yes. Suhni took my hand and led me inside the cottage. Everything was made of dark brown wood. The colors comforted me. She led me to a corner of the room to a bed. I crawled in. The sheets smelled like musk. Suhni stroked my hair. "Tell me a story," I said to her, my words slurring. She smiled and began to sing:

Long were the nights once, full of terror and longing
Clutching my aching heart, each night I cried

I longed for my love, for my Mehar, for freedom
I longed to hold his hand in mine and to ride away
To lands unknown to anyone but us
And to forget anything and anyone we knew
But every day his absence tormented me
Until one day I dared
To cross the violent river
Days it took me, days
To build up the courage and strength
But Mehar's voice called me
And his strength became my strength
And …

Sleep took over me again. Her beautiful voice carried on singing but I could not make out the words. I willed myself to understand, I needed to know what happened. I forced myself awake and listened—she was talking about her sister-in-law:

Oh, my husband's sister
I do not blame her, she loved her brother
Or perhaps my Mehar, I can not know
I can not hate a woman who harms another
And says it is out of love
For I did the same, I did the same
And when I was sinking, then I prayed
Let my Mehar find me, God,
Let my Mehar find me
I called him to me with all my heart
My last dying breath was his name

Again, I fell asleep. The last words I heard were:

And he found me

I woke one day here in this house
And moments later came Mehar

When I woke up I was still in the dream, in Suhni's bed. The house was empty, Suhni and Mehar were nowhere to be seen.

I stepped out of the door and the space outside where the fire burned, which was empty last night except for seaweed and passing fish, was crowded with the men and women and children who had been swept up by the flood. There was a feast. People were sitting in long files, cross legged on the seabed, on either side of a long white *dastarkhan*. They laughed and ate and joked with one another like one big family. From a distance I saw Suhni, glowing golden in her beauty. I began walking towards her but was stopped by a kind-looking woman, a mother, I believe, who smiled at me and took hold of my hand. She made me sit next to her on the *dastarkhan*. All kinds of foods were in front of me, but none of them were meat. A plate was passed to me. A laugh escaped my mouth, but it might have been a sob. I helped myself to some *salan and roti*. On land, we had built cities and factories and forgotten our fishermen. But the Sea had not. It was still their Sustainer.

8

Protection Spells Against Long Covid and ME/CFS & When My Long Covid and ME/CFS End Me, Will a Mudang be Waiting?

POETRY

M.S. Marquart

Protection Spells Against Long Covid and ME/CFS

Tigers were in all of our *halabeogi's* bedtime stories

when my brother and I visited Korea with our mom.
He was our only relative there who spoke English,
so *halmeoni* fed us steamed rice and salty grilled fish,
and our step-grandfather told us about going for chilly night walks
in the green-smelling woods, where he would always meet a tiger.

How are you enjoying your grandchildren?
the tiger would ask in a growl. It knew we were visiting,
because it was always watching over us,
even when we were on the other side of the Pacific.

It made sense: in our California home,
a carved wooden tiger stood guard, fangs bared.
I loved to stroke its soothing, smooth shape, and feel
protected.
I believed in those tiger stories longer than I believed in
Santa,
but then the wooden tiger disappeared after I went to
college,
and my memories of halabeogi's stories faded.

My friend Rebecca has brought back those memories.
She sends me tigers:
Tiger lamp, tiger print, tiger plush toy
that can flip from happy to fierce.

We share a Korean American heritage,
and with these tigers, she is sending me
the symbolism of power, strength, and peace.
She is sending me sacred guardians
to protect against evil,
to actively chase away bad luck.

Being so cared for brings tears to my eyes.
I put the tiger lamp next to my side of the bed
in the corner of the studio apartment I share with my husband.
The low white glow of the tiger's body
watches over me, giving me strength.

With my severe disabilities, every day is a battle.
She understands, and I feel her constant care.
She wants to chase away my struggles;
she wishes me luck with my health.

I put the tiger plush toy below the tv, facing the couch.
When I don't have the energy to eat,
when I can't stand up to go to the bathroom,
when my brain fog prevents getting anything done,
when I spiral into worry and despair,
I look up to see it watching me,
encouraging me, and I take a breath.

I've been waiting to hang the tiger print, but it's time.
During Japan's colonization of Korea,
tigers were a symbol of resistance, courage, and hope.
After the 2024 election, the fear and dread are constant,
and it feels like I need these tigers, bearers of my friend's
love,
reminders of my ancestors' protection, now more than ever.

When My Long Covid and ME/CFS End Me, Will a Mudang be Waiting?

On my sickest days, I squint through my brain's fog
at the outline of a woman dressed in a loose white hanbok,
long, wide, flowing sleeves, matching white-winged cloth cap.
Ceremonial drums thump and little golden bells chime,
faint in the distance.

I wonder if somehow I can freeze time, to send one quick
final
message to all the people I love before the mudang
guides me to the afterlife.

Then I wonder whether as a half-Korean,
raised in the United States,
who doesn't speak the language,
I have the right to be guided to the next world
by a Korean shamaness, a leader of Korea's official indigenous religion.
Am I Korean enough?

However …
sometimes they are called halmeoni — grandmother —
to show greater respect than the title of mudang.
For more than 4,000 years, most Korean shamans
have been women, working for female clients, and women's
work
is scorned all over the world, especially when it pre-dates
formal education.

I had a halmeoni in Korea, ate her specialty grilled galchi
fish and rice,

played nights of goduri with her hwatu card deck, listened to bedtime
stories from her English-speaking second husband, fell asleep on her padded floors
to the smoky chemical scent of green mosquito repellent coils slowly burning to ash
while a fan rotated hot summer air over me and my brother.

I had a great-halmeoni in Korea, always dressed in traditional hanboks,
with hair tight in a bun and the most wrinkles I had ever seen on a human being.
We bowed deeply to her when we visited her traditional countryside compound,
with pointy wooden eaves where swallows nested, rice-paper sliding doors,
and an old-fashioned hole-in-a-wooden-platform toilet to squat over
while my mother held my arm so my little body didn't fall in.
Her husband had passed away, and she ruled the household strictly, but always seemed happy
to see us. We communicated in smiles, gestures, bows, and nods,
and her calloused waxy hand gently cupping my face. I learned how to say
in Korean, "I'm very full, thank you;" she had survived Korea's occupations and wars,
scarcity and inhumanity, and she kept feeding us, her great-grandchildren.

So ...
if mudangs are sometimes called halmeoni, and I had two halmeonis,

maybe a mudang will guide me to the afterlife one day after
all. Maybe shamanism
and mudangs are already entering my subconscious —
mudangs show people
the unseen powers behind nature, the spirits in every object
on earth and in the sky,
the connections between people and the cosmos.

Since my disabilities have made me homebound, nature's
magic
has become ever-more obvious. Could a shaman be guiding
me as I look
out the window, track the progress of the trees' leaves, watch
the birds play?
As I eagerly seek out green buds outdoors while inside I plant
seeds in old tuna jars
and gasp at the sparks of wonder in my chest every time a
bud bursts into bloom
mere weeks later? How can only dirt, sun, and water be
enough to create life?
I can see the shamanistic perspective that spirits are everywhere, impacting everything.

How else to explain the way the calendula flower captures
the color of the sun?
How else to explain the way that tulip petals become ever-
more beautiful as they age,
colors deepening as the petals wrinkle, shrink, curl?
How else to explain the way that a trip to a field of wildflowers, a tree-lined lake,
or a chilly beach can create a forever-oasis in my memory?
Maybe a mudang will explain all this on my final journey.

9

Hearing Voices
NONFICTION
Angela Yuriko Smith

Growing up, I was cautioned against speaking with spirits. I was told our family in Okinawa had been yuta before migrating to Hawaii. The women in my family were afraid of this ability. We shared dreams. We ignored the voices speaking with us. We tried to pretend we were normal.

Yuta are traditional Okinawan spirit mediums who serve as intermediaries between the living and the spiritual realm, often called upon to resolve issues related to health, family, or unexplained misfortune. Predominantly women, yuta are not formally trained but are chosen through a spiritual awakening known as kami daari, a divine calling that may manifest through dreams, illness, or powerful visions. It's a curse if you don't survive it, a gift if you do.

All yuta have some form of a spirit voice, a form of communication from ancestral spirits or unseen forces, which may be heard as an inner voice, a vivid dream, or a deep intuitive knowing. Guided by this voice, yuta interpret the will of the spirits and helps restore harmony between people and the world beyond. Despite modern skepticism, yuta continue to play a vital role in Okinawan cultural and spiritual life, blending indigenous beliefs with elements of Buddhism and Shinto.

I think my voice has always been with me. It-she-they would tell me things I needed to know—*don't trust that grownup, leave the playground now, don't climb into that empty fridge and close the lid*. Sometimes in dreams, sometimes in a voice that seemed audible to my ears, sometimes a wordless nudge in the back of my mind, later, I came to call my onboard guidance system simply "the universe."

Whatever they called it, I know my mother and grandmother also had their own voice, but they reacted with dread and denial. The last time I spoke with my grandmother, who I was named after, she refused to turn off the radio evangelists, hoping that their constant static petitions would drown out the call. Instead of offerings of awamori, rice and fruit to our ancestors she sent paper checks to snake-tongued salesmen of spirit.

My grandmother was one of 12 children. Of that generation I only met her and her brother, Shigaru, Uncle Shige to me, and later Uncle Sugar to my first daughter. He worked for the CIA as a cryptographer and had once had to make his way on foot out of Russia. He was a man of high intelligence and exotic ways, a man of great importance. I knew this because he was the only man my parents allowed to smoke in our house. He was a man who had traveled the world, collected elephant carvings and had been declared dead twice. I met him once, but we were penpals from when I was a teen to when he finally passed in 2015. Through his letters, I learned about the world.

About a year after he passed, he had one last adventure to share with me. His guidance would set me up on my own journey into self-acceptance. Strange things began happening everywhere I went. I couldn't explain, and neither could those who witnessed them.

I walked through the kitchen and a blender would start up. The television did the same thing, suddenly blaring full blast all on its own. I spooked my boss. I wasn't spooked. There was some normal explanation we just didn't have access to.

Then, at home, things got intense. Instead of just turning on, things started blowing up. Our microwave shorted out with a loud pop when heating up a bowl of ramen. Our electric oven did the same, giving off an unexplainable bang before dying. The next morning I went out to our locked garage to find all four of my tires were flat. No problem, because I also had a moped scooter, but both tires were flat there too. Desperate to get to work on time, I hopped on to my bike, which thankfully had full tires … until I was within sight of my workplace and then they both suddenly went flat.

As I wheeled my bike back home after work that day, I gave serious thought to what was happening. Logic and reality had left the building. In the past, when I tried to tell well meaning people about strange things, I was told I was crazy. I was institutionalized for a few months and put on medication to help me stay grounded in reality. But this time, there was a stack of faulty electrical appliances as proof that something, indeed, was strange and perhaps it wasn't my imagination after all.

What would a yuta do in this situation? I asked my inner voice

The answer was to listen, somehow, without my ears. To see without my eyes.

And there was my Uncle, disoriented in the spirit world. He was bumping around like a drunk, confused by the state he was in. He realized he was no longer physical, he realized he was now loose from his aged flesh, but he couldn't figure out how to maneuver himself. He was stuck in our house, trapped when he still had so much world to see.

How do I help him? I asked without words.

Make him a small feast, I was told without words.

I filled a small bowl with rice, soy sauce and furikake. I poured a glass of liquor. I carried the small meal along with a cigarette and some incense sticks to the front porch. I arranged it all in front of the open front door so he would see it and come out. I lit the cigarette, blew a few puffs into the house and propped it up. I lit the incense. I spoke with Uncle Shige. I hoped my neighbors weren't watching.

Uncle, I love you but it isn't good for either of us if you stay here in my house. You want to see more of the world, and I want the peace of my house back. Follow the smell of cigarettes and bourbon. Come, enjoy what I've prepared for you. This doesn't mean you can never come back. You are always welcome here.

I could feel his spirit moving through the house. He was following his nose, sniffing the burning tobacco. I could feel a dry pricking in my throat and I imagined that's what he felt, thirsty for bourbon. He hesitated just inside the door and then he came through. I couldn't see him with my eyes, but I knew he was there. He enjoyed the small feast I'd made him, but after a minute he was agitated again. I realized I was still blocking his path, and I almost fell off the porch trying to clear his path. My uncle passed by.

Nothing more happened to us after that. Electronics stopped turning on by themselves when I passed by. Things stopped blowing up. Our tires stayed inflated. But I was different. Instead of pretending to be blind I had allowed myself to communicate with a spirit. It happened to be a loved one and it brought us both happiness. On one hand, I was raised to think spirits were all demonic tricksters laying in wait to snatch careless souls for eternal damnation. On the other hand, I helped my uncle to continue his journey. I couldn't see why that was wrong.

From that experience, I opened my mind to consider that

perhaps what was unseen with the eyes was just as valid, possibly more valid, then was my brain perceived as reality. I couldn't see germs either, or wind, but they affected me regardless. I began my research.

I wanted to know all about yuta and what my family did before Hawaii, but the information was hard to come by. When my uncle was alive I had attempted to ask him but his answer was cryptic. "Don't speak of the past or the past might come back to haunt you." But here he now was, a spirit from my past, and I had spoken with him. I didn't feel haunted.

I searched for yuta, for any news, any leads. In the absence of connecting with yuta I studied all the other occult practices and knowledge I could find. I learned, I practiced, I kept copious notes. Then, in late 2021, everything started connecting.

On impulse, Lee Murray, Christina Sng, Geneve Flynn and I decided to write *Tortured Willows*, a poetry collection on our Asian heritage. I felt like an imposter. I didn't know Okinawans were not Japanese until I was 30. Okinawans are a separate people with a distinct culture and language known as Shimanchu, Ryukyuan and/or Uchinaanchu. I am only a quarter Uchinaanchu. I didn't even know what Uchinaanchu was until I started researching for the poetry collection. How could I write about my heritage when all I had are some strange stories and even stranger experiences?

Suddenly, the world cracked open and I started finding leads and information on a daily basis. Unrelated, my younger daughter moved to Brazil and we found much of the information I'd been searching for is in Brazil. I followed her there on impulse. Like I could feel Uncle Shige moving through my house, I could feel a pull to move to Latin America. It was the right choice, but since I started taking my inner voice seriously, it always is.

Here I am now, and I have never been happier. I no longer live in fear. When things go bump in the night, I ask them why and then help them go bump somewhere else.

Sometimes I wonder if I'm yuta now, or a witch, or something else entirely? I use both Google and tarot cards to plan my weekend. I listen to my friends on both sides of the veil. I navigate by map app and pendulum. I hear voices and am better for it.

10

Ingredients Instead
FICTION
Ayida Shonibar

When the cold creeps into my bones, I struggle to dispel it. I'm not built for a climate like this—ice gouging sharp fingers into my skin, dry winds snatching the breath from inside my lungs. As I sink into my office chair, even my colleague overhears my joints moaning in their unhappy sockets.

He watches me burrow into my throw blanket knowingly. "It comes with age. Your body's slowly giving up."

I don't think it's my brief tenure on Earth exacerbating my condition. But I cannot possibly explain to him what is.

AT HOME, I flip through the battered, dog-eared notebook that's been sitting on my kitchen table for the last year, untouched. My finger traces over the arcs and flourishes of the Bengali script.

Since childhood, the same aches and fatigue have descended upon my body like a flock of vultures in the winters. My parents had moved me across the world at an age I hardly recall. My shorir knew, though, at every down-turn of the season. It rebelled at being uprooted, trans-planted to somewhere it didn't choose to belong. Fevers overtook my physiology. Coughs conquered my vocal cords. I might have been my family's obedient little baby, but my constitution had a will of its own.

Struggling to take care of us on unfamiliar ground, Maa confided in my grandma, who flew over to look after us as our matriarch. She brought with her the family's old rannar boi, passed down from her own mother. It was a ruled note-book, filled with handwritten instructions and lists, fading analogue photographs taped inside.

Long after my grandma returned home, Maa continued poring over her recipes. My sore throats were soothed with spiced ginger tea. Headaches lifted by the lightest of mushur dals. The freeze in my organic matter thawed out by the heat in pepper-infused gravy.

I was fine then, while Maa was still here to distil our family's alchemy.

The tightness from my skeleton spreads into my tear ducts. Her loss continues to linger fresh in the sinews of my anatomy.

My hands keep following the Brahmic letters inked by one of my ancestors. I form the shape of the curves, go over the lines.

It's the closest I'll get to knowing them.

THE PICTURES HELP. I remember Maa assembling ingredients, pouring things into our vast clay pot in a care-fully sequenced choreography.

I emulate parts of her craft. My brew bubbles in her coral-coloured cauldron, wafting my favourite scents of coriander and chillies into the air. I measure things as best as I can, relying on cups and scales and spoons I never once saw Maa resort to.

This is the way I was taught to understand cooking.

The cold-banishing maacher jhaal throws me for a loop. One of the key components, shorsher tel, isn't obtainable here.

Without it, the rest of my preparations appear meaningless.

Frustration bubbles up into my sinuses. It burns, smarting through my nerves and making my eyes water. The corrosive feeling channels through my skull, leaks onto my face, and drips into the pot.

The simmering gravy turns golden. A pungent fragrance rises from the mixture. It smells as acerbic as my emotions, effervescent and reminiscent of mustard. I swirl the wooden spoon through the aromatics and blend the salmon pieces in.

Even the fish is the wrong type.

I WORRY my ingredient substitutions render this dish an utter failing of my ancestral heritage. The first spoonful doesn't taste anything like the meals Maa would prepare, but a few bites in, sensation floods back into my extremities and warmth suffuses my cheeks.

Something in my system comes to life.

Halfway through my plate, the recollections trickle in.

They're not mine. Just like my body remembering a homeland my episodic memory doesn't possess, my tongue deciphers history from the spell-matter that binds the ingredients together.

My mother's grandma, who survived a famine, living in a time and place that made scarce the materials her ancestors had relied on. Where staple crops were meant to effloresce, plants uprooted to build infrastructure for colonial enterprise. Harvests yielding necessary food items, only to be loaded onto foreign ships and sailed off into the horizon.

My great-grandma, barely a grown woman, persisting.

The notes she wrote so painstakingly for her recipes were logs of experiments, iterations of manipulating missing variables until, at last, a magical combination came together to heal the pains her family struggled to overcome. The hurt had settled deep into her own bones, documenting her experiences, passing biologically rendered records onto grandchildren who would carry them without ever being able to read their inscriptions unless they were to flay themselves open to inspect their insides.

I swallow the last of our meal and wash up.

Once everything has been cleared away, I place a neon sticky note into my family's book, beside the photo of the spicy hot fish curry.

My English letters are cramped and inelegant as I jot down the changes I made. For someone else to find and remember.

11

Worry Wah Wahs
FICTION

Frances Lu-Pai Ippolito

"Someone told you it was worth a lot?" The shopgirl asked when she glanced at the wedding ring I'd set down on a stack of the Daily Chinese World Journal. She spoke with her mouth full and I saw her teeth grinding boba before her lips sealed back around the end of a fat yellow straw. She slurped and then slurped some more, her cheeks hollowing as brown tapioca balls traveled up the plastic tube on a flow of milk tea.

"Yeah, how much?" It had to be worth thousands, but I didn't need the best deal; just somewhere quiet to unload before Jonathan's lawyer added personal assets to the divorce settlement.

"Da Jie, ni bu yao le?" Big sis, you don't want it? She said this in Chinese and I wondered if she was more comfortable in a native tongue or, perhaps, it'd be more intimate to ask a "sister" where I'd gotten the ring.

"Bu yao." No. I switched even though I knew I couldn't keep up. My American Born Chinese was shit—barely enough to ask for what I needed but never enough to give anything useful in return. But I wanted to play along. Maybe

58

she'd give me a better deal if we were distant "family" rather than strangers.

She slipped my wedding ring over her finger and tilted it into the light. The ring sparkled, a brilliance dancing off sharpened edges of cut diamond. I expected it to look beautiful, but the ring's white light made the girl's hand look a dirty yellow. She was better off without it, as she was, in braided pigtails down to her waist and an oversized pink Hello Kitty sweatshirt.

Had I been better off too? Before Jonathan?

"It's too bad—" she shook her head and sighed. "—it's only worth $20."

My breath hitched. "No way! It has to be worth hundreds if not thousands," I insisted, unable to keep the desperation from slipping in.

Her gaze darted between me and the ring. The inkiness of her eyes darkened as a mixture of suspicion and curiosity passed over her plump, young face. I was sure I'd become a pathetic puzzle to her. Here I was in designer clothes, full make-up, and hair permed straight—like the sophisticated Asian women on the glossy magazines racked behind the register—only to be pawning jewelry for quick cash.

"It's not worth much to me." She dropped the ring on the stack of newspapers. It fell but didn't rest, spinning around newspaper headlines until it stuttered to a stop, much like my heart had in my chest.

Of course, the Was-band had lied about this too. Just like everything else in the marriage. "This is the last time, I promise. No more affairs." *Now, what'll we do?* I placed a hand over the tiny bump below my waist. *Don't worry, I want you.*

"You know, I'm going to do you a favor," the girl said suddenly, startling me by how close her face was to mine. "Wait here." She jogged around the counter, disappearing down an aisle of hanging pots and pans, and out through a backdoor.

I stood for a moment, staring at the place where she'd gone. *What was I doing here?* The Shop was a dusty, forgotten place, too dull to compete with the Daiso or 99 Ranch across the street in the trendy Asian strip mall. Piles of Chinese magazines and books lined the shelves next to mahjong sets, Sanrio stationery, and underwear and slippers stuffed into protective crinkly plastic bags. Loose red envelopes for Lunar New Year and weddings were spread across the counter next to the newspapers. I set my hand on an envelope, letting my fingertips trace the raised characters 喜喜 for marital bliss.

I should take the ring and go. This kid couldn't be more than early twenties and here I was, someone old enough to be her mother, hoping she had an answer to a divorce, frozen bank accounts, and a secret pregnancy. *I'm not ashamed of you,* I whispered inside. *You're a secret because he wouldn't want you. We'd get in the way of his new life, new wife.*

But I stayed and waited as the minutes ticked by because, honestly, where would I go? I had nowhere but that single room in the Golden Palace Motel on Atlantic where the $80 a night bought me a bed, a locked door, and a nightly carpet of roaches.

The girl reappeared at the door, struggling to hold a large cardboard box. The box looked barely intact with three of the flaps dangling half-torn and the bottom corners of the box worn and dotted with peek-a-boo holes. Shorter than me, her arms slipped and the box almost crashed to the ground before she stooped to gain purchase.

I rushed over. "Let me." I tried to take the box from her. She batted my hands away and clutched on.

"You help me?" She huffed and studied my abdomen. "Who's going to help you?" She nudged me back with her elbow, gently despite the tartness in her tone. I stepped back, giving her space. She cracked her neck, rolled her shoulders, and dropped the box to the ground. A plume of dust rose out of the box into the air. She bent over and began dragging the box by its one good flap to the register counter, like a mother tugging on a naughty child's ear.

"What is it?" I looked over her shoulder. A tendril of childish excitement unfurled in my chest like a fern frond. It'd been a long while since I'd had any good surprises.

Her chin lifted and amusement flashed in her eyes. "Go ahead, see for yourself."

I pulled back the other flaps and peeked in. Several clear eyes peered up at me. Dolls. Dozens of dolls. Barbies, babies, Bo-Peep, and others old, young, shapely, or somewhere in-between. They all stared at me with glassy eyes that didn't blink.

"Wh-what are these?"

"Worry Wahs-Wahs."

"What?"

She used her index finger to turn over one of the flaps. The characters " 娃 娃 " were written in black ink across the top.

"That doesn't help. I-I can't read Chinese," I admitted. Face burning.

"Wah-Wahs. They take your worries away. Just tell them what's bothering you at night before you go to sleep. You'll feel a lot better after. Go ahead, pick a couple. My treat. They're all wonderful, but I suggest the one in the sweatshirt. She's the most experienced at fixing worries. She's one of a pair of sister dolls that my mother specifically made for that purpose."

"Is this some kind of joke?" My chest tightened as burning anger churned in the pit of my stomach.

"No, not at all. Mama was a puppeteer and toymaker," she said as if that made any more sense to me. "The sweat-shirted one is the best, but the rest are fine too. Mama didn't make those, but she repaired them. The only downside to sweatshirt girl is that she's the *second* cutest. Her sister is cuter." The shopgirl winked and then giggled, a bubbly sound like water running over river rocks.

"Ha. Ha. That's real funny." I reached across the counter and palmed my ring. This kid sucked. The Shop sucked. And I was ready to leave, except a wave of nausea washed over me and I retched, quickly covering my mouth with my hands.

The girl jumped around the counter and handed me the trash can. I threw up, breakfast, lunch, and whatever was left of yesterday's dinner. Collapsing on my knees, I buried my face into the trash can.

"It's ok," she said beside me, rubbing my back, and holding up my hair. It was so soft and comforting, the way that my Po-Po used to touch me, that I couldn't hold back the emotions anymore. Tears slid down my cheeks.

"I'm sorry," I mumbled when I could breathe again.

She handed me tissues. "For what?" I felt her watching me as I wiped my mouth.

"For losing it. Making a mess. I haven't been able to sleep much since . . . ." I palmed my belly and tried to stand up. My legs were weak and I wobbled before a reed-thin, but steady arm shot out and caught me by the waist. The girl was tiny, but she had a vice-like grip. "Uh, thanks."

"I have something that'll help." She let me go once I'd grabbed a hold of the counter and draped myself across for support. Pigtails bounced as the Shopgirl ducked behind the counter and dug below the cash register. Her head popped back up like a chipmunk's and she handed me a bundle of incense sticks. Sandalwood filled my nose, blocking out the lingering scent of vomit and bile.

"Burn them when you talk to the Worry Wahs-Wahs. It'll help with the nausea."

"Thanks, but I don't think I can buy these—"

"I'll give you $500 for the ring if you take the incense and the box of dolls," she said, cutting me off.

"You just said the ring's not worth anything."

"It's not. $20 for the ring and $480 to take all the dolls and incense. I've got a lot of clutter and you'd be doing me a favor."

Favor? The whole place was clutter. This was charity, but I was too desperate to reject it. Head hung low, I said, "Ok."

She grunted in approval and placed the incense sticks in the box, ready to carry the whole lot to my car.

I HATED DOLLS AS A CHILD. Never played with them. Was always afraid they pretended to be dead while the world was awake. Still felt the same at forty-three. And the only reason I'd brought the box into Room 14 at the Golden Palace was the slim chance that the Bo-Peep doll I saw buried under Malibu Barbie was vintage and saleable on eBay.

I reached into the box and pulled out a doll by the long, thick ponytail. Not the Bo-Peep, but a chubby-cheeked little girl that reminded me of an American Girl doll. Blunt bangs tickled her eyes and a dimpled smile gave her a cute, impish face. She wore baggy jeans and a white sweatshirt that said "You're special" in bubblegum font. This was probably the one that the Shopgirl said was the "best." I set her beside me to look back in the box for Bo-Peep.

A knock sounded at the door. I scrambled to get off the bed and tuck my blouse back into my skirt. Before I could get to the peephole, I heard a key slide in and the door opened.

"Oh, you're here," the motel manager, Mitch, stood in the doorway.

"Yes, I just got back." I eyed the "Do Not Disturb" placard hanging from my door. *Was the man coming into my room whenever I was out?*

"You complained about roaches?" He lifted a bottle of Raid in his meaty hand and looked at me. Well, he looked at my chest and my legs. He hardly ever made eye contact. "I came to spray."

"That's not enough. They're everywhere." The bottle was the kind used for a couple of bugs here and there. Every night, hundreds of roaches of all shapes and sizes came out to scavenge my room. They scaled the walls, ceilings, closet shelves, floor, even crawling on my blankets and weaving into my hair. A few times, I'd woken up for the bathroom only to squish several dozen on the way.

"Ah, sweetheart, are you scared of bugs?" Mitch strode into the room to stand right next to me, so close that I could feel the heat of his skin pressing against mine. He was a few inches taller than me and I could follow the direction of his stare directly into the V-neck of my white button-up. The roaches were gross, but I almost wished a few would climb out of my shirt and jump at him.

"You know, I've always liked Asian women." He wagged his brows at me and I felt the urgency to throw up again.

I forced a swallow. "Uh, Mitch, I'm not feeling well. Could you come by tomorrow instead?"

"Busy, huh? You sure you don't need my help?" He lowered the Raid and rested the can on his crotch. "I thought we should help each other out. I gave you a pretty good discount for the week's stay."

"I'm sorry, I—" I couldn't finish as I threw up in my hands and ran to the bathroom sink.

"Shit! You are sick! Better not be contagious!" Mitch

tossed the can on the bed and ran out the door, slamming it behind him.

Jerk. I hobbled back to the bed and reached into the box for the incense. I dropped a stick onto a used plate and lit it. Not fire safe at all, but my stomach immediately calmed to the sandalwood. I sat back down on the bed and fingered the cash stuffed in my skirt pocket. If I were still the wife of Jonathan-the-Anesthesiologist, I'd tell off Mitch-the-Fucker and find a better place to stay. But I had nowhere else to go. Pawning the ring was supposed to get me out of the motel. The $500 wouldn't get me much more than 2-3 nights somewhere slightly better.

Oh, wait, the Bo-Peep. I reached in the box again and pushed through crinoline, plush, and jersey shirt fabric to find a bonneted blonde head with clear green eyes and pouty pink lips. Straight out of a storybook, Bo-Peep wore a paisley skirt draped over a fluffy white petticoat. A snug black vest criss crossed over a cream-colored blouse with puffed sleeves. A Shepherd's crook rested in her left hand. I picked her up and flipped her around and brushed aside her bonnet ties and blonde curls to expose the nape of her neck. "娃 娃"was scratched into the rubber skin. Wah-Wah. Quickly, I sat her down on the bed next to Ms. Special as I googled the Bo-Peep on my phone.

I groaned when I found a similar doll on eBay. $21 dollars. That's it.

I flopped onto the bed and stared at the popcorn ceiling. A fat roach clung to the bowled light fixture. A mother by the size of the turgid egg sac attached to her rear.

"I wish this place were cleaner. Wouldn't be so bad if the roaches weren't everywhere," I said to Bo-Peep.

As I watched the pregnant bug, I palmed the can of Raid that had rolled toward the dip I created in the saggy mattress. I wrapped my fingers tight around it until my knuckles turned white. All I had to do was stand on the bed and spray. The roach and all her babies would die. But I didn't. I laid there watching her struggle on the smooth hot surface. It was the wrong time of day and wrong place altogether, making her too easy a target. Like me. Fuck . . . my life analogized perfectly to a pregnant roach in a seedy motel. I let go of the can and let it roll away off the edge of the bed. Didn't feel like collecting bad karma today. I flipped the switch by the bed and turned off the ceiling light.

Suddenly, fatigue seeped into my bones. It was only 6pm and summer sunlight streamed through the fibers of the threadbare curtains drawn closed at the only window in the room. I hadn't eaten yet, but the thought of food made me gag until sandalwood wafted by and chased the urge away. The things we mothers do for you, I thought to the blip in my belly as I settled my head into the pillow and shut my eyes. In my drowsy mind, I continued to watch the roach climb a burning sphere of light, secretly hoping she'd find her way to wherever it was she was going. "I want us to be safe," I murmured.

When I woke, the room was dark except for the glow of the streetlight filtered through the curtains. *Must have slept a few hours.* I sat up and my bladder jabbed back, painfully full. I swept my hand over the wall to switch the light on, steeling myself for the sight of roaches scurrying to dark hiding places. But when the light came on, there were none. I blinked to adjust my eyes. Not a single one. Not one to question good fortune, especially on a bursting bladder, I hurried to the bathroom and shut the door.

Through the bathroom wall, I heard a knock at the room door.

"Just a minute!" I called out and then hesitated. Who could that be? It was late. Then I heard the door open.

"Wheeeeere you at Tiiiiiinaanananaa?" a man's voice slurred.

Mitch. He sounded drunk. I stood quickly and pulled up my panties. I'd slipped off and left my skirt by the bed. My phone was charging there too, out of reach.

"T-T-T-Tina, you T-T-T-Tease," he called.

There was a thump and loud crash as if he'd stumbled and fallen over something like a table or chair.

"Oooh, Tina, Tina, Bo-Bina," he sang. "You've been holding out on me. Look likes you got some money here after all."

Shit! He was going to take the only cash I had left to feed myself and my blip with. I grabbed a dirty towel off the floor and wrapped it around my waist.

"Mitch," I said quietly through the bathroom door. "I'm still really sick. And you don't sound too good. Why don't you head back to your room and we can figure out stuff tomorrow?" I tried to keep my voice level even though my bare legs were shaking underneath the terrycloth.

"There you are!" Mitch said at the gap under the bathroom door. "Found you! Now COME OUT!" He banged on the bottom of the door and stuck his fingers through the gap.

My hands flew to my mouth and I started to cry softly. I closed my eyes and whispered to blip, "I just want to keep you safe."

"Ow, fuck!" Mitch yelled, pounding angrily on the door. "Tina, you know you can't have any animals in this room! Your fucking dog bit me!"

Dog?

"Tina, you asked for it. Once I find that little fucker, I'm going wring its neck and then sue the shit out of you unless you convince me not to."

I heard him stomp away from the door and chase something across the room. "I got you now!" Glass shattered followed by the sounds of furniture overturning. "Fuck! Fuck! What the Fuck!" Mitch screamed, no longer sounding angry but . . .frightened. "Get away from me!" He shouted once more before the room was silent.

After several minutes, I opened the door a crack and peered outside. The room was a disaster—table upended, chair legs broken, and the box of dolls crushed flat. Mitch was gone.

I'm getting the hell out of here. I'll sleep in the car. I zipped on my skirt, grabbed my bag and stuffed the few clothes and toiletries I had into it. I grabbed keys and started out the door and nearly tripped when an arm grabbed my waist.

Mitch had been standing on the other side of the door, waiting for me. I struggled against his grip as he pushed me back into the room and locked the door.

"Got you to come out, didn't I? Tina, you're going to pay for this," he said, raising his palm to show a curved row of bleeding indentations. "Your dog might have gotten away, but not you." I twisted in his hold as he wrapped both arms around my chest and slipped a hand into my blouse. His fingers pinched at my skin.

"Stop it! Let me go! I'll scream!"

He threw me against the wall. "Go ahead. You think anyone around here is going to take your side? They're even more desperate than you. And they know how to keep me happy." He drew closer and I shuffled backwards.

"Aren't you a little old to be playing with dolls?" Mitch tilted his head to Bo-Peep, Ms. Special, Malibu Barbie, and a few more glass-eyed baby dolls who sat on the carpet, sand-wiched between us. *Had he taken them out and arranged them? God, he was a real sicko and I was trapped in here with him.*

"Please don't hurt me. Take the money. All of it. I just want to leave." I pulled the wad of cash from my pocket and tossed it at his feet.

He grinned. "Sugar, I'm taking this money and some extra hotel fees." He crept a few steps nearer and lifted a foot to step over Ms. Sweatshirt Special. Then he tripped and fell hard—flat on his front side.

"What the hell?" he said, lifting his face to look right into Ms. Sweatshirt Special. She almost appeared to look directly back at him with the same bright smile and perky ponytail. A roach crawled out of her nose hole.

"Gaahh! That's disgusting!" Mitch jumped up.

More roaches crawled out from Ms. Special. Out of her ears, her hair, the joints of her limbs, and her shiny smile. Hundreds poured out of her doll body—all heading straight for Mitch.

He tried to stomp on them as a moving sheet of twitching antennae raced for his feet. He kicked at them, hopping frantically, slapping his sleeves and at his skin to knock the roaches off his body. He smashed a few, but the roaches were too many. They charged into his nose, ears, and eyes. Mitch screamed and ran in circles in the room. Whenever he opened his mouth, he choked on the roaches burrowing into his throat. His teeth clamped down, crushing bodies in-between. But when Mitch gagged, more roaches surged in. There was no way for him to fight the large unified mass storming onto his face. His eyes bulged. He sputtered, spat, and foamed at the mouth. Finally, he collapsed to his knees, to his chest, and stilled.

For a long time, I sat by the wall, hugging my knees to my chest, rocking.

"Mitch?" I whispered finally. Mitch laid face down, his mouth agape and eyes wide open staring at ceiling. The lingering roaches that hadn't gone into him, scattering off to their hiding places behind the walls.

I edged closer and nudged his shoulder with my toe.

He didn't move.

Oh God, he's dead! I had to call the police, I thought as I backed away toward the door to my bag and phone. I saw a flash of movement and turned around in case Mitch had gotten up.

Mitch was still on the ground, but Ms. Special sat in her same spot with one difference—she now held five folded $100 dollar bills in her hand. Next to her, incense sticks were laid out in a line.

"WASN'T it lucky he had a heart-attack, then?" That's what the police officer said when the coroner came to pick up Mitch's body.

"Will you be staying nearby?" the police officer had asked me after they packed everything up. "I'm assuming you won't be staying here."

"Uh, I think so."

"Well, stay safe out there and we'll call you when we need more information."

"Ok, thanks," I waved from my car as they drove out of the parking lot.

I started the car, circled the block, then the city, aimlessly driving until at dawn, I found myself at The Shop again. It was barely 5:30am, but the light was on and the Shopgirl was there by the counter.

"Good morning Tina," the Shopgirl said as I walked in with an armful of dolls. I hadn't told her my name the day before. She didn't look up as she continued to speak.

"Mama was a master puppeteer. Dolls came to life in her shows. After one show, a rich man came to Mama's house and demanded to marry her daughter. She told him she was childless and there was no daughter he could have. But he insisted that he'd seen her in the show—a beautiful girl with long, silky black hair and round cheeks. The girl was young and innocent; the way he liked it. Mama explained many times that she didn't have a daughter and each time she did, the man grew angrier until he hit Mama with his hand." The Shopgirl paused.

"And then?" I heard myself say.

The Shopgirl sighed. "She fell and hit her head. Never woke up before she died."

"The man?"

The Shopgirl looked up at me. "The man did what some men do. He lied. Called her a sorceress, a witch, who'd made him fall in love and lose his mind. Self-defense. There were no witnesses."

"But she had a daughter? You. Couldn't you tell them what happened?"

The Shopgirl's pink lips quirked up into a sad small smile. She turned her body and lifted her braids to show the nape of her neck. Imprinted on her flesh were the words "娃 娃."

"Mama didn't have a real daughter. But she was my mother just the same."

12

We Feed the Hungry Ghost
FICTION

T. S. Ren

In October, when the viscous membrane between the spirit world and ours thins, my mom sends me a text. "Daddy is home, come home for dinner one day?"

My father left us when I was in high school. He said he left to start a business, but really he left because he was bored. He was bored of driving rich people around, bored of my mother, bored of his three children, and he was hungry. He wanted more: more money, more control, more children, more women, so he flew south to make a new life for himself. He comes back to haunt us on special occasions like the holidays or his friends' birthdays, or when the veil between his world and ours becomes porous.

SINCE HIS TRANSFORMATION into a hungry ghost or an e gui, he spends most of his hours roaming the docks of Florida in search of seafood and women.

So I take advantage of this rare sighting and head to Flushing for dinner with him, his friends, and mom.

· · ·

MY MOM PICKS me up from the train station. "Isn't that shirt too low?"

I look down at myself. "You bought this for me."

"Whatever, too late to change now."

I ADJUST my shirt and follow her into the restaurant, past empty tables and tanks that are more animal than water: a crush of tuna, a knot of eels. My father is waiting for us, leaning against the door for support. His belly is distended from beer, his limbs thinned from diabetes.

AS HE MOVES to hug me, I brace myself for a hand to settle at the small of my back, or my ass, but his hands pass through me. It feels as though a cold front has engulfed my arms and I shudder. "Hi baby. Are you cold?" my father asks.

"Hi baba, missed you. No, I'm ok."

His hair is a silver helmet that sits atop his head like that of a medieval cavalryman. Every time he comes back to haunt us, he gets smaller, more stooped, the rigor mortis more pronounced in his leg.

SITTING at the roundtable are the usual suspects. There's Bill, the proprietor of a Chinese language bookstore in Flushing. He has a shock of gray hair and an innocuous face that belongs to a chipmunk cartoon. Next to him is Chen Shufu, who used to teach my father kungfu back when he was still with us. He has eyebrows bushy enough to rival those of the Chinese God of War, and he drapes a bear's coat over his shoulders. Their wives sit across from them: Brown bob and Gray bob. They have the same wrinkles in their heart shaped faces, their bobs chopped off at the same severe angle.

My father says, "Why don't you sit next to aiyi over there?"

Mom and I sit next to the women. My father sits across from us, next to Bill and Chen Shufu. Conscious of my shirt, of the men in the room, of my father across me, I fan my hair in front of my chest like a curtain.

IN HONOR of the hungry ghost, we order a shit ton of food.

Dishes come out in a procession: green beans tossed with mala and glistening pork, sliced beef and pig ear, spare ribs roasted red and sweet, salted peanuts with flaking exoskeletons. My mother will never hug me as tight as I'd like her to nor will she ever say she's proud of me, but she leaves offerings of dou miao on my plate like leafy love notes. Waiters bring in a stained clay pot of soup, an entire headless chicken and herbs simmering inside, along with a bowl of shredded tofu skin, wood ear, and shrimp. Next, a junkyard of disembodied crab legs, reassembled and topped with a shell, a mimicry of a standing crustacean, of what once scuttled about the shores of Maryland.

FOR A HUNGRY GHOST, nothing will ever really be enough. Not this food, not us, not the whole of New York City. My father cracks crab legs with his molars and gnaws on spare ribs as if they were an ear of corn.

ALL THE WHILE, Bill opens an urn and, instead of ash, he pours out shot after shot after shot of baijiu. Chen Shufu calls over a waiter to help open a bottle of Cabernet which he offers to the women.

HE STANDS, the bottle hovering over my cup.

I smile and say *no thank you* in Mandarin. My father rarely invites us to these meals with his boys (it's a boys' only club, with the exception of everyone else's wives) but when I do go, I only need a handful of Chinese phrases to get by. *No thank you* is one of them but there's also: *yes, thank you, I'm the eldest, I'm 27, work is busy but good.*

Chen Shufu says, "Aren't you your father's daughter? ███, why not have some!" Sometimes my grasp on Mandarin is like an overexposed photograph with black holes burned into an otherwise intact scene.

"No thank you," I repeat.

"Just a little bit then," he says as he tips the bottle into my cup.

"Ganbei," everyone holds up their glass and clinks them together. Instead of drinking, I wet my lips with the wine.

MY MOTHER SPOONS lima beans on my plate and their tender insides burst in my mouth, all green and rich oil, the kind men chase and die for.

I've tuned out most of the men's conversation and the aunties' Shanghainese tittering, but I hear my father crow, "If someone treated me so well, they can hit my butt whenever they want!"

AROUND HIM, my father's friends laugh like a Greek chorus, and he, gracious patriarch, lifts his glass up. Baijiu sloshes and spills on his hand, on the yellow tablecloth, and it glistens like lighter fluid underneath the fluorescent lighting of our private dining room.

"Who's hitting whose butt?" Brown bob asks.

My father says, "Aiya, ok, ████, so you know I was in Taiwan earlier this year, me, the wife, and my younger daughter. She's moving too slow, so I hit her butt, you know to make her go faster, and she was furious. Didn't talk to me for 2 weeks."

I CANNOT UNDERSTAND the full story in his rapid Mandarin, but I know it intimately from my sister's point of view. I know that while they were traveling in Asia together, he kept slapping her butt, and that this moment was the last straw for her. I know she yelled at him and the weeks of silence between them yawned like a dark chasm. I know that this is not even close to being the first incident, and that when she has told him to stop in the past, he'd act like it was a joke and would do it more, harder.

There is little my sister and I keep from each other, but I don't know if she wants to know this: the way he tells this story to her grandmother and his friends as a joke, turning her into a horse he can kick to go faster. It sits in my throat like the pit of a cherry I've swallowed. I try to wash it down with chrysanthemum tea to no avail.

I KNOW that my father has slapped my butt too when I'm passing by him watching war documentaries or drug cartel dramas, on family vacations when I make the mistake of strolling in front of him. I know that from the age of 8 to 16, he'd call me sexy in English. In his accent, it is a cross between "sexy" and "sassy", but I know in my bones he meant the former every time. The precise pitch and rhythm of it coming on his tongue haunts me still. I know he has another girl with another woman, and maybe I should resent her, resent that she gets to spend more time with my dad than me, but I don't. I'm scared for her because, while he might know how to be a parent to young girls, he left us before he could learn how to parent adults.

MY MOTHER, of all people, comes to my sister's defense. She turns to Brown bob and Gray bob and says, "You know, she's 21 now, ████████████ and he sees her as a kid—you know how easy that is for a parent to do."

My father ignores her. "She doesn't talk to me for weeks, but she still uses my credit card. If someone lets me use their money, they can hit my butt however much they want!" He waves a crab leg in a spanking motion, and little garlic pieces fly off. "Gan bei!"

THEY'VE POLISHED off the urn and have moved onto the Cabernet.

"Wah, you didn't drink any of your wine! Why not?" Bill asks me.

My mother takes my glass. "She just doesn't like drinking," she says before she sips at the wine.

"Who's driving home?" I ask her. I bite into the Lion's Head meatballs, which dissolve in my mouth, leaving oil, fat, and the crisp crunch of water chestnut and scallions.

She looks at my father, wine dribbling onto the tablecloth like blood. "I'll drive, don't worry."

"But you've been drinking."

"Aiya, don't worry, this is just wine, it's nothing."

"Ok, fine." I take my glass back and down the wine. It goes down like Nyquil, sour and unforgiving.

"Ah, you're just like your dad after all!" Chen Shufu crows. He rubs himself under the table and I sneak a concerned glance at him and relax. He's just massaging his arm.

"Without your dad, you should not drink, but you can drink and relax now!" In Bill's mouth, it has the symmetry of a Chinese proverb. "Because your dad is here to take care of you!"

My mother rubs her eyes as if she's crying. I know if I ask her if she's crying, or if she's okay, she will evade the question so instead I ask her if she's enjoying the food.

She avoids my eyes as she nods.

Bill moves to open another bottle of wine.

"Wait," my mom says. "I think we're done drinking now, you don't want any more, do you?" The aunties shake their heads. "███████████. I'm driving so I'm good. Maybe we shouldn't open up another bottle if we can't finish it."

"Are you sure you don't want more?"

I pull my cup away. "No thank you."

"Oh come on, just a little more!" Chen Shufu takes the bottle and cracks it open. Gray bob looks at him, a sneer on her lips. "Why do you need to drink?"

"We're just having fun! ███████████."

"You need to drink to have fun? We just finished that other bottle, we told you we're not drinking anymore." Gray bob switches into Shanghainese and continues firing off. I stare at the massacre on our white plates, carcasses of crabs and shrimp heads, pig ear cartilage, the shells of peanuts and lima beans. A fly lingers on new territory, a plane of sliced beef.

"Ok, one more," my mom concedes after Bill pours me and her another glass of wine. "Remember I'm driving you back home tonight too."

. . .

DESSERT IS BROUGHT OUT, sliced watermelon as crisp as an autumn day, and sweet fried potato buns with "luck" 福 stamped on its side.

FOR THE REST OF DINNER, I watch my mother's hand, which once played guitar, once slapped me and all my siblings, once cooked sweet yam for us, once smoothed our feverish foreheads, once slammed car doors, and once carried groceries. That same hand becomes an umbrella over her cup, hovering over it in case Bill swoops in with another glass.

AS I WATCH HER HAND, I am 13 again. My father is still with us, and we're in the thick of a swampy summer in Shanghai. We have been at dinner with my father's friends for hours. We have been watching them empty bottles and bottles of baijiu, my father flushing the color of oxblood. He morphs into a mercurial spirit, at moments shouting and others laughing boisterously with his friends. He snarls when my mom asks if he's had enough and when I say I'm tired and bored and want to sleep.

I AM 13 and I devise a game for me and my siblings. The objective is to get Daddy to stop drinking. I make Jessica, who's 7, grab the bottles of alcohol and run away with it, hiding it behind the curtains. Brian, who's 6, spits watermelon seeds into the adults' glasses. And then Daddy roars in a voice that ripples across the white table which opens up like a sea between us. He yells at Jessica to fetch him the bottles back and then he downs the baijiu, watermelon seeds and all. He smacks his lips as he looks us dead in the eyes.

MY MOTHER IS TAPPING ME, and my eyes focus back on the fly hovering over the meat. "Come on, let's go home. Help your dad, make sure he doesn't trip."

I offer my arm to my father, but he gestures for me to go ahead in front of him. I tense up as his hand reaches for me, forgetting, for a second, that he is a ghost.

13

Don't Forget Me

FICTION

Kristy Park Kulski

Halmoni watches me eat, her eyes sad, the glitter of tears making the delicate capillaries shine a little more red against the dulling white sclera. The lines of age deepen, hair growing even more gray with her sorrow. Her lips move. Whispers so faint they seem mere puffs of air, meanings that collapse between us and fall into nothingness, like incense in the wind. Like a life that never started.

At first, she frightened me. Her staring like an endless ache following each mouthful. Back then she had been solid, seemingly real and less of the wisp of a dream. But now it seems she's grown barely substantial, flickering in and out of my peripheral vision like an interrupted projector image. Always present, but not always visible. In the velvet dimness of the small apartment, her sobs flit like gnats in and out of my awareness.

I miss her, yet I wish for peace too. It is a terrible fight within my heart. A push and pull that drives me to insanity.

Why does she do this to me, her granddaughter? I, who loved her best. For the child she raised. And while I am not yet an adult, I am old enough to be on my own—a teenager and only months away from graduation. She must let go. If we must be parted, let us be parted. Because it hurts too much to be reminded, she is not with me—not really. Not in the ways it matters most right now.

I try to forget her, to move on. One cannot stay in one place forever. Aching in my helplessness to be anything useful to her, to never get the chance to see her at my graduation beaming with pride—as she would have. She's beyond my help and her tears are the taste of everything I've lost. Of what could have been.

HALMONI LINGERS most often at mealtimes. Her attention is like an itch, a thing squirming from the shadows, soon it grows in intensity—stretching toward me. Her need forms an icicle piercing my core. Over time, I've learned to try to ignore it—but trying and doing are not the same thing. The shine of her eyes flash in the gloom and for a moment there she is, small and translucent in a white hanbok.

Now, she sits in a corner, rocking herself as I devour rice cakes and fresh-made stews. Keeping vigil even as I suck the meat from crab shells, chew the center of calms. I sip rice punch and warily keep watch like a deer sensing the tingle of threat in the air. Yet, warmth blooms in my heart, an ache that makes me want to reach out too. But the hunger will not tolerate any halt in consuming my meal, not until every bite is gone.

Memories of school meander through my mind, as does the sense of duty. But even in these thoughts, the brown-gray of this apartment remains. This place must have had a beginning and therefore it will have an end. But its cavern is a belt that tightens and leaves those of us trapped inside breathless and hopeless.

BEFORE WHEN IT *went from normal to ending completely. There were doctors, lots of them. Cancer they had said. Halmoni reeled and my heart ached. She shouldn't have had to go through it. It's not fair. The days were long. The nights were longer. It was just the two of us and the gloom.*

THE NEXT MEALTIME COMES. As usual, I leave no dish untasted. Nothing untested or unappreciated. But the hunger seems more intense, everything within me is tight with it until I hum with need. I eat as if I've never eaten before. I eat as if my memories could be digested.

Halmoni weeps.

I am unsure if she is driven to watch over my nighttime feasts out of joy, or if my grandmother is simply jealous that I can relish food. Perhaps she isn't able to eat in the world she inhabits.

"Halmoni," I call out. Her flickering slows and she lifts her head. "I know you are there."

She doesn't answer. She never does. But I know she hears. "You don't have to take care of me anymore. It's okay to move on," I urge between mouthfuls.

Her sorrow makes the room contract like a womb trying to spit me out. How much longer I will be able to tolerate this, I do not know.

Halmoni has begun to rub her hands together in a circle, bending her back, hovering over any spark of energy she might raise. Before, I would have fetched her a blanket to keep warm. I would have brought tea.

But she's too far away now.

She won't stop chanting.

Soon, I can only turn over in my dreams wishing for peace.

THE SHAMANS SAY when we die, we return to the earth. We become soil, rejoined to Grandmother Mago whose body is the Earth. They say, we must return from which we came, into the bits and pieces that formed us. We fall apart but not in a distressing way, in a way that seems natural. Like the release of a long held sigh. That our spirits are air and our consciousness can dance upon the wind and in the voices of others. We could become a song or the cool water that refreshes thirsty children.

The Buddhists burn their dead and find beautiful pearls of purity within the ashes of the holiest. Beads of sanctity. Proof of a life of virtue, of the highest awareness.

There are stories that tell of spirits reanimating the newly dead. Some are fox spirits who do this, some are dead people too, and some are both.

This shaman arrives with pursed lips, leaving her shoes by the door and inspecting the apartment. I can sense the power within her, the energy of her communions with many spirits. Her spine keeps her upright and proud. Knowledge sits comfortably upon her shoulders and heart. Relief fills me and for a moment the hunger quiets in her presence.

I tell the shaman about my grandmother. Tell her about the sobs and the watching. She listens, eyes sharp, nodding as we go.

When I finish, the shaman breathes deeply, as if awakening.

She calls out to my grandmother. Her voice is firm but not unkind. A woman who is used to giving little quarter.

"Go now," she tells Halmoni. "You must stop watching the child eat. It bothers her."

There are no drums as would be seen during an elaborate ceremony, no loudness or frenzied energy. I am thankful for the informality and the silence. But before the shaman leaves, she writes a sigil in red upon yellow paper. Thick marks of her brush, heavy and light swirl into a connection of almost characters and seemingly random shapes and lines. Power emanates from them the moment she lifts her brush. She pins this one and many like it above doors and windows. It is then I notice for the first time, she is replacing another of the same with the newly drawn ones. Talismans everywhere in the apartment.

"Just in case," the shaman says.

I AM hopeful for tonight's meal. To finally be left in peace. A pile of beautiful fat pears and stacked rice cakes stuffed with sweet paste adorn the low table. In front is a cup of milk, fresh and well-chilled. The hunger I feel is like nothing else. It is as if I have never eaten a meal. For a moment I reflect with gratitude at the bounty.

The shuffle of cloth forces me to turn my attention, and I see a flash of Halmoni's slippers disappearing around a corner. Away. She is leaving me in peace. It worked. It really worked. At the same time, my heart sinks a little. Regret that I would drive her away like this. But the heaviness of her presence filled with yearning and need has departed and I can for the first time enjoy my meal. I am giddy.

I eat the rice cakes first.

IT IS after the third solitary meal, I grow bored. The apartment has always been too small but Halmoni and I had never had much money for anything bigger. I recall walking to school; the memory is odd and disjointed. I realize I haven't been to school for a long time. Would my friends remember me at all? Surely, there is an assignment I should have completed. Something I should have studied. A lightning bolt of curiosity hits me. Where have my school things gone? Flitting throughout I search drawers and cabinets and finally discover—stuffed into the back of a closet, my school bag. A layer of dust has settled into the cracks of the fiber. My prized collection of charms looks to have been unclipped and is missing from the zipper.

I dig more, there are layers of things. *My things*. The closet stacked full of it. Old clothing, photos, my favorite doll from when I was little. Plushies too, only a couple but the charms are nowhere to be seen. Searching and searching, I don't stop until I've emptied it out. But the charms are gone. Halmoni always said to retrace our steps when we lose something important to us, that usually what we have lost is simply waiting for us to find it.

I think, the last time—I barely remember but, I would have been walking home from school. Perhaps they fell off.

Maybe it's just a process of going outside to search. I reach, pulling at the front door.

The knob doesn't twist, instead it feels like one solid piece under my fingers. Unyielding, as if it was never made to respond to touch, like solid stone. I try again, harder. Still there is nothing. Above, the talisman paper seems to flutter in an odd breeze, flashing red and yellow as if laughing.

I open my mouth to voice my frustration, but only the tiniest whine escapes. As if something has swallowed my voice.

Then the hunger returns. So fierce I crumble to the floor and cry.

FROM THE BEDROOM, I hear Halmoni's cough emerge like a plume of dust in lamplight. The shaman steps out. I am observing from the corners, questions and hunger hissing from my being, but I do not speak. Her eyes turn in my direction, adjusting to the dim light, but she sees me. She startles, then her expression softens.

"There you are," the shaman says. "Where have you been all this time?"

Her question makes me feel as if I've done something wrong. I blink trying to understand how to answer. *Where have I been?* Right here. She should know. *Why doesn't she know?* I'm always right here.

"Why can't I open the door?" I ask, pointing to the talisman. I know it's because of those but can't say how and in what way to express exactly why it would matter at all. I can't understand why she would do this, trap me inside. It is not what I asked for. The only thing I had wanted was for Halmoni to stop shadowing my every step and bite.

"Your grandmother didn't want you to leave without her," the shaman explains. "She was afraid you wouldn't find your way."

"I just want to find my charms," I counter. "I think I lost them coming home from school."

Another cough echoes through the apartment. The shaman half turns to peer into the room, dark hair lank around her drooping shoulders.

"You will understand soon," she says to me. "Go eat. I know you are hungry."

THE TABLE IS LESS full than I'm used to but it's enough for now. A photo set up in the corner slows me, tickling something … a reminder, something I've forgotten perhaps. It is of me, smiling on my first day of school. *Cancer they had said.* I am excited to find a handful of melon flavored candy.

For a moment, I miss Halmoni.

WE REMEMBER *the making of the world, the waking of the Grandmother Mago. We keep the songs and the keeping of these memories, of these histories is the cold quiet power that resides in the deep recesses of the Earth. It is the quiet latent hand of emergence that pushes the plants and trees upward toward the Celestials. We remember that it is death and its leftover that garner life in the first place.*

We sing of her in our rituals. We tell the stories just as we cast out sickness. We draw the lines, the precise brushstroke of our protection rites with her song on our lips. You've heard them talk in the West of the witches who were burned, they who have returned. Old souls in new bodies. But burning is to send a thing to the spirit world. Burning gives more power to the powerless. And nothing about the past is in the past.

It is all now and here.

My hands are small and wizened. The lines of many songs. Of children I have held, the sick I have nursed, the dead I have buried and mourned. When the tears fall on the curled tiger, its children far and wide know the sound of the dew falling from the heavens upon the mountains. It is merely the patter of the sea joining the sea.

HALMONI EMBRACES ME, more than just arms and heart to heart, she holds me with her entire being. I don't understand, but I'm not afraid. She's different. Or maybe I am the one who is different. I cannot tell. The shaman chants in the bedroom.

But all I can think is—*Halmoni is hugging me. Halmoni is hugging me.*

I hug her back with everything I am. An ache rises in the air, the pieces of my loneliness and her loneliness meeting again. We grab ahold of those pieces as we grab ahold of one another, clinging to the safety it brings. She whispers with joy at the sight of me and the ache melts into cool water and song.

"I've missed you," she says over and over.

The shaman has placed a fresh plate of sweet rice cakes on the table with burning incense. Halmoni and I gather together, hand in hand. We are hungry, but the pangs are soft, no longer the pain of absolute emptiness. We take our meal together. She pats me and beams, a bright and shining thread of love. I smile back.

Everything is alright, I think. And I feel settled, as if a decision being agonized over has finally been made.

A bustle from the bedroom results in a group of men emerging with a figure swathed in cloth from head to toe. They maneuver around the doorway and the tight space of the apartment and out the front door.

A body. Halmoni's body.

The shaman follows but stops short of leaving, giving Halmoni and I a look of understanding, of assuredness. "Be with Grandmother Mago," she intones.

"It is done," Halmoni tells me.

"What is done?" I say.

"Life," the shaman answers, moving to the talisman over the door, pulling it down. "It is time for you both to return."

"It is a journey," Halmoni says, gazing down at me. "I

didn't want you to take it alone. I am here now. We will go together."

"Leave?"

"Yes," Halmoni says. "To finally leave."

"I'm ready," I say, and I suddenly—realize how lost I'd been. That she sensed it. With Halmoni here with me, I won't get lost again.

I nod. "Melon candy is my favorite," I say.

"I know." Halmoni gives me a smile, bright and beautiful. "I always put out your favorite things for jesa."

I sigh long, like the wind blows through me. Regret is replaced with peace, hunger with purpose. "You didn't forget me."

"Never." Halmoni squeezes my hand.

We step forward together and walk through the door and out of the apartment—into the smoke of incense— and into the songs and cool waters of the world.

Just the sea rejoining the sea.

14

Windows

NONFICTION

Theresa Drew Falk

For my daughter, Rebecca Lourdes, and for her Lola, Lourdes Miranda

Heart of Mary, Quezon City, September 2013

In the shimmering midday heat, in the courtyard behind the chapel, I walk beside your tiny form: just enough space between us to hint that I am now yours and you are now mine.

I do not reach for your hand at first. Sister Lorens, seemingly no bigger than you, holds it instead. We walk through the grass in large, solemn circles, a labyrinth leading to the future. As we walk I wonder about our ancestors. Are they watching now? Have they gathered to witness this joining? Will Mayari bless it with her moonlight?

Each step feels oddly light, like I am floating above the muddy ground. I look up and into the eyes of The Blessed Mother, gazing at me from a statue as I walk by. Her hands are stretched outward toward us. When I was a little girl, your Lola Lourdes would pray to the Virgin Mary every

91

night, asking for support in raising her difficult and strong-willed daughter. She would pray to her for patience as I unleashed my American guile. As I spoke to her in disrespectful thunder peals. As I stomped away from her, turning my back. I look over to you, wondering if you will do the same.

"It is inevitable, you know."

I turn toward the voice, thinking it is Sister Lorens, but she continues to face forward, guiding you along the cyclical path. Above her head I see The Blessed Mother, white hands now folded gently in front of her, smiling knowingly at me.

"All mothers and daughters walk the same path."

"I don't know where this goes," I whisper. "I don't know which direction is right."

"It's not your decision, *anak*. It is hers. You can only walk with her as she goes."

As if in answer to Mother Mary's words, Sister Lorens beckons to me in a smooth but declarative swish of her hand. Without breaking our stride, she moves aside, placing my palm to yours for the very first time. For a moment she wraps her small hands around both of ours and squeezes, as if to seal us together. I look back toward Mother Mary. She has returned to her original position, but her arms now feel open just for me.

You are so small, yet I do not feel big. The weight of new motherhood bursts upon me with a blinding, painful light. For a few steps you do not notice that this is a new hand in yours, and you continue to gaze at the heavily pregnant cat lying on her back against the nursery wall, licking her full teats. It occurs to me that I will not be able to nurse you. Although I have considered this before, the pain of this realization drops into me like lead.

I was born in 1969 to a white woman and Filipino man.

Both were married to other people at the time of my conception. They gave me up, and I was adopted by your Grandpa Brand and Lola Lourdes, who raised me, nurtured me, and loved me until their deaths and beyond.

Your Lola Lourdes taught me by example that a woman's power lay in her ability to not only love, but to recognize the magic that exists in the world: between people, between humans and the earth, and between the spirits that inhabit it. The fact that a half white, half Filipina child found a home with adoptive parents who exactly matched her ethnic background–in 1969 Los Angeles–has never felt like a coincidence to me. It has always been, and always will be, proof of the sacred warp and weft of the universe. I wasn't theirs for a reason. I was just theirs.

But are you mine?

On the way back to our Makati hotel, in the back of a yellow taxicab, I hold you firmly in my lap. You look up at me with glassy, wondering eyes, and I tighten my grip as we navigate the bumpy Quezon City streets. My American stomach churns as our driver weaves fearlessly through the pattern of roads, but you laugh and reach for the windows, gazing out. These are your roads, and these trees, these buildings, these murals along the walls, this dripping heat and sonorous chatter belong to you and not me. I want you to look at me, to see me, so I dangle a piece of White Rabbit candy before your little nose, and you take your hand off the window to grasp it greedily.

"Do not fear her light, *anak*."

We lurch to a halt next to a colorful muraled wall, from which a female figure dressed in bright sunflower yellow steps out into the sun. One moment she is paint, and the next she is beside me, raising a glowing hand.

Hanan. The Morning Goddess. The Goddess of Light.

"What if she does not love me?" I whisper.

"Her light will shine in all directions. Sometimes it will seem to hide, but it will always find you."

"What if I can't find me?"

Hanan's hands meet, glowing against her belly.

"Light finds light, daughter," she says, and the taxicab drives away. Hanan's eyes follow us until we round the corner.

Your Lola may or may not have walked these streets. She never told me the entire story.

I can only remember slivers shared over coffee and eclairs. She stole candy to survive during World War II: only pieces small enough to fit in her pockets. I imagine her hungry and frightened, wandering these same streets, running from soldiers and missing a mother she never really knew. Did she smell these same smells and feel this same sun as she crouched behind buildings, unwrapping her candies, quietly trying to stay alive?

I wonder how she got to the docks that day in 1950. Was she dropped off by a friend or did she take a car? Did she walk the last mile with a suitcase in her hand imagining the life she would one day lead? Did she try to picture the Naval officer she would meet in a Los Feliz coffee shop and marry, and cook stew for, and eventually mourn?

Did she imagine me?

She had no idea that over sixty years later another Lourdes would find her way—that her wide-eyed *apo* would clutch at her new mother's hair and press her tiny hand to the window of a taxicab that would also take her to America: to Hershey bars and coffee shops and maybe even true love.

The three of us do not share blood. We will not share a physical space in this life. But the threads between us are not invisible. They glow golden, magenta, and turquoise, woven in strength and beauty, a living textile of our love.

I think of all these things as I hold you on my lap, watching you take in a landscape that you will soon leave behind. I put my hand over yours, pressing it firmly into the window. I know for a fact that hands reach out to touch you from the other side.

15

Rule of Threes
FICTION
Arushi Karthik

Stella D'Silva believed in the absolute. She believed in solid things like the walls of her church, the water that filled the Anjuna River, or the tide that came in and out without fail at the shore. Things had to be real– to be seen or heard, to believe in them. So she disregarded the old wives' tales of the rakondar, bhuts, and especially of the evil eye. Fairytales belonged in books, and the stories she'd been told as a child seemed like nothing more than soft threats to make children behave. But the boils that appeared on her baby's skin were very much real, and so were the screams that left her wanting to do something– *anything* to make his pain go away. The child was only two days old, and it felt like too young an age for someone to feel anything, let alone pain.

The doctors' salves, tonics, and the numerous injections did nothing. Instead, red splotches joined his skin in between the black boils. So they brought the child home, where at least he was surrounded by only Stella and Francis, instead of strangers. Stella gave up believing in the absolute and science fairly quickly, and sent her husband to fetch a voijinn maim, one of the traditional healers who removed the evil eye. He found none in Anjuna, nor in Vagator, nor in Calangute. Even in the little towns that rested between, Francis found no one.

She had remembered the voijinn maim during her childhood in the small village of Paloli. But they were not in her village, and voijinn maim had long before left behind the cities in Goa. The world had poured into Goa, and like the rocks on the shore, time and influence had worn away some of their old practices, their cultures. Anjuna seemed foreign to even Stella at times, so crowded with tourists and visitors. The city was filled with people of different colors, a majority of them wearing the characteristic khaki shorts and the air of infrequent showers. Anjuna had become a place where there were more hotels and hostels than homes, and so no one ever really felt at home.

Stella aped the rituals she had seen a thousand times. She gathered the dry red chilies, the herbs, the lemons, and performed the ritual as well as she remembered it. She stumbled upon tribal prayers offered by women over the tribal prayers that the women offered. The words were foreign on her tongue, the prayer so different from her usual hymns and recitations of the bible. But she did repeat them, more fervently than any of her prayers before, and continued until her voice was hoarse. Her child healed. Like magic, the boils disappeared overnight, and Stella's belief in the absolute crumbled at the corners. She ignored how she felt a little bit different from before, how her reality now seemed to be spinning on a tilted axis.

To celebrate the child's recovery, Francis brought home pomfret and fenni. She cooked xacuti with the fish and had a few sips of the coconut liquor while Francis indulged in half the bottle. He stumbled into bed while Stella settled down in their living room to feed the baby. Francis's happiness came easier to him, because he understood the baby's recovery even less than she did. He did not know enough to be unsure of their miracle, to question whether it was only temporary.

She heard the door to their bedroom close, and assumed that it was only Francis. Feeding the baby was not loud, but it was not silent. Their son was healthier now, and clearly audible whether he was gurgling or crying.

"So, did you enjoy playing the part of a voijin maim?"

Stella turned, and saw no one. Her living room was dark, and infinite things could hide in the shadows of the old home. The windows were open, and the fronds of the coconut trees were dark stripes against the lilac sky outside.

"Who's there?" she asked. It was a woman's voice, so soft it was nearly a hiss.

"I am the one who cast the nodor on your child," the voice said, and Stella heard the smile on the stranger's lips. "An evil eye to put a quick end to a short life. Until you decided to do something which you were not supposed to do."

"I only did what others do," Stella said, her voice steel and her arms tight around her child. She had seen countless others ward off the evil eye. There was a reason the voijinn maim were so rare. They were slowly disappearing into the forests, one by one.

"Sometimes the red chilies, the lemons, the salt, and all those other household remedies are enough to ward off an evil spirit. Not in this case," the voice said. "You drew on powers you had no right to. You stepped out of your boundaries, which gives me permission to step out of mine."

"Show yourself!" Stella yelled. She was tempted to call on her religion, but had the feeling the voice did not operate by the laws she had been taught to follow in church.

"Do you know what voijinn maim means, Mrs. D'Silva?" the voice asked. "What they are meant to do?"

Stella did not know. She did speak Konkani, but the

language was more colloquial, the language she used for buying groceries and sharing gossip. She used words without fully knowing their meanings, just like many around her.

"The world operates in threes, Mrs. D'Silva. Heaven, earth, and the under. Good, human, and evil. The voijinn maim—a protector, a mother like you—a creator, and those like me—the destroyers. You have upset that balance, Mrs. D'Silva. In the natural order of things, your role was only to grieve."

Finally, a woman rose out of the shadows. Her dark hair was in a long and thick braid, and her lips were painted bright red. She smiled, like she held more secrets behind them than the grains of sand on the shore. Her saree was one of gossamer, and the darkness hid more of her body than the cloth.

"You are a witch," Stella said. "A dayan."

"The world operates in threes, Mrs. D'Silva," the witch said. "And so I have come."

The living room clock rang three times, and Stella looked away for a moment. When she looked back, the bundle in her arms was only cloth, and the witch was holding her child. She held him like he was not a life, but an inconvenience.

"We must reset the balance, Mrs. D'Silva," the witch said.

"If you do something to my son …"

"Your son did not upset the balance, Mrs. D'Silva," the witch said. "You did."

"What are you saying?"

"I am saying that you have played two roles out of three," the witch said. "And now you must play the third. Place a curse of your own. Become a dayan. Make some other woman grieve, if she cannot find a voijinn maim."

16

Ancestral Rituals is Cultural Reinvention

NONFICTION

Pauline Chow

At first, rituals felt like a blend of play and self-care. I didn't expect that burning candles, hiding stones into my wallet, and shuffling tarot cards would open a portal to my ancestors. Like many millennials searching for meaning during the hard times, I spiraled into social media and landed in the spell-laced world of #WitchTok. The practices I found were mostly Eurocentric, but they stirred deeper questions. As I lit candles and whispered intentions, I began to hear echoes:

- *Where are the witches in my culture?*
- *What magic had my ancestors practiced before it was forgotten?*
- *And what would it mean to reclaim that knowledge and remake it for the modern world?*

Erasure provokes. In the United States, the call for "simpler times" resonates through different dialects. One political side is dragging the country backwards towards a mythologized version of the 20th century, a so-called gilded age. Supporters rally to worship rigid gender roles and racial hierarchies, honoring a narrow definition of humanity. Meanwhile, witches are digging into ancient times, invoking ancient divine feminine figures to instruct, inspire, and initiate. They call upon Hecate from 800 BCE, Lillith from 2000 BCE, and Shiva from 400-200 BCE to help remake our chaos into something more compassionate and flexible.

Growing up Chinese American, the culture of my home often clashed with the outside world. My first-grade teacher told my parents to stop speaking Chinese with me. For a time, educators claimed bilingualism hindered cognitive development. My parents understood the nonsense of denying my heritage and pushed me to flourish in both Cantonese and Mandarin. I did pretty well in school too. Without their wise decision making, I wouldn't have experienced the pleasure of cross-generational Hong Kong family dramas or tried out for the coveted Chicago Chinatown nomination for Miss International Hong Kong. (Spoiler, I didn't win.) The ability to speak multiple languages and live between cultures creates an innate ability to simultaneously hold multiple worlds in my heart.

The conflict with language in a mixed generational household is mild compared to the explosive fights about sleep-overs, wearing make-up, and dating. Cultural clashes bit deeper into my core. I wasn't just being a moody teenager. I ached to confirm my belonging and identity. A western way of life seemed to offer more freedoms and opportunities to reach a higher potential that weren't afforded to the females in my lineage. My maternal great-grandmother was the last to have her foot bound. My grandmother stayed loyal to an abusive arranged marriage. I that that if I leaned too hard into the old ways, then I couldn't progress.

Confucianism is embedded into my heritage. The foundations of the philosophy subordinates the feminine to fathers, husbands, and sons. It is part of who I was going to become.

I cast my first spells with a writing coven. High Priestess Lindsay Merbaum hosts classes with a detailed syllabus and prompts on witchy topics. From cannibalism to shapeshifters, the High Priestess guides the group with short stories, academic articles, and electric discussions. During the October Witch session, I journaled my darkest secrets inside a salt circle. Then I called upon Medusa to reflect my true self in a cup of water.

I feared turning to stone when facing my real self.

MY MATERNAL GRANDMOTHER had laid out chopsticks, steaming bowls of rice, and a whole boiled chicken during full moons in the agricultural calendar. The floppy neck of the pale carcass stared into the room with hollow eyes. This dead animal and the prayers locked in my childish curiosity. Why did she fuss over dead people? They were already gone.

Her rituals would take all day. Incense filled up a small room next to a yellowish, seventies style kitchen. At sunset my grandmother whispered to the darkening horizon and poured liquor into the garden beds. These actions, so quiet and so seemingly futile, didn't sparkle like Sunday Church with a five-piece band or Christmas Mass with costumes and plumes of Frankincense.

Ancestral worship is a staple in Asian cultures and tightly wound with filial piety. As I distanced from Confucianism, I also loosened ties with my ancestors. I assumed ancestral rituals were uneducated superstitions that could never rise to the level of magic.

But then I lost my job, twice in nine months. Both times I pulled The Tower card from my tarot deck the week before the news came. The first time I shrugged. The second time I cried with happiness.

Amidst the chaos of these jobless times, my mother proposed a pause.

In February 2025, I flew to Hong Kong for a job fair and visited my grandmother's ancestral village. When the timing is right, you just say yes to everything and go.

Returning to Hong Kong where my parents grew up felt like drinking a warm bowl of soup on a rainy day. The moment the plane touched down, doubts about who I am melted away. Between speaking three languages in a single breath and indulging in meals that taste like memory, my body and brain enter a state of ease. It was more than nostalgia. It was a recalibration.

Before I could continue my exploration into mainland China I needed an additional stamp on my Visa. While I waited, I read Nancy Hendrickson's books on *Ancestral Tarot* and *Ancestral Grimoire*. Since I couldn't rush into the second part of the trip, I was given the insight to connect to my ancestors by blood, land, and time. Later, I completed Benebell Wen's course on discovering the "Ancient One," an inner archetype rooted in ancestral lineage. These frameworks grounded me into ancestral practices without my former cultural baggage.

Then it happened. I got the stamp that I needed to enter China. I traveled by high-speed rail to Taishan, the city of my grandmother's birth, for the first time. While I had traveled to Hong Kong frequently, I had held onto the image of my grandmother's village as rural and impoverished. My maternal family stems from the Pearl River Delta, a name that signaled a paradise. But the narratives of peasantry stood fast in the image of my family's ancestral home. The idea was so strong that I even doubted my grandmother's stories of dancing, singing lessons, and competing in high school volleyball tournaments. This changed when I visited a museum in Taishan.

Photos and artifacts from the early 1900s displayed a vibrant and sophisticated time. Schools and communities had incorporated international concepts, built trains, promoted the arts, and designed balconied avenues. My grandmother hadn't exaggerated. The Taishan Girl's teams were renowned in playing volleyball.

The impromptu trip shifted my mindset from desperation to worthiness. I stopped centering my family history around struggle and suffering. My ancestors were innovators and adventurers. I had assumed healing meant releasing and forgetting the past. Looking at my reflection in this shared history didn't turn my flesh into stone. I had found a new way to forge a future.

Now, my ancestors are integral to my daily rituals. Dressing my altar with offerings of honey, pinecones, and wildflowers brings history into the present. Ancestors are our co-creators. Seeking answers from them is a form of reverence, an intimate act of magic.

When we honor the past and live fully in the present we channel power into the future. Transcendence is integration. Witches don't allow erasure and oppression to get in their way. We call out to resurrect the dead. We create magic from the mundane. We find the treasures buried deep inside of us.

17

Bewitched by K-pop
HIGH-STAKES RITUAL MAGIC FOR MODERN WITCHES, NONFICTION

Chaweon Koo

K-pop isn't just entertainment—it's one of the most successful magical operations ever executed. Behind the polished choreography and catchy hooks lies a template for high-stakes ritual that transformed a war-torn, economically struggling nation into a global cultural superpower. While most witches busy themselves with aesthetic TikTok spells, South Korea has been demonstrating real-world magic that reshapes reality.

After the 1997 IMF crisis, Korea faced an existential threat. Their economy crumbled. Their future darkened. What emerged wasn't just cute pop groups, but national survival magic; rituals that *had* to work or their country would slide back into poverty. Most modern witchcraft, by comparison, is low-stakes dabbling.

The Ritual Theater of Transformation

When BTS takes the stage at a world tour, they create specialized magical spaces. Reality suspends. Time warps. This is what a proper magic circle was always meant to be—

not some chalk outline, but a charged container where energy, consciousness, and intention manifest powerfully.

The lights, costumes, choreography, and staging aren't mere aesthetic superficiality. They function as technological interfaces generating collective hypnosis. Meanwhile, your altar sits collecting dust. You haven't approached your rituals with the same dramatic commitment and intensity.

Western magical traditions have sanitized ritual. We walk politely around circles, hips stiff. We mumble Latin and arcane dialects and non-colloquial, high-falutin' scripts. Meanwhile, K-pop idols dance until they collapse, channel intense emotions, transform energetic patterns through somatic practice. They revive the ecstatic, embodied magic our ancestors understood intuitively.

Magical Components Hidden in Plain Sight

K-pop's magical system can be broken down into specific components that witches should study:

Sigils & Symbols: K-pop groups don't just have logos; they wield charged sigils that encapsulate their essence. BTS's bulletproof shield. BLACKPINK's stark emblem. These aren't random graphics but condensed magical intent repeated across platforms. Light sticks function as ritual wands, binding thousands of fans into collective spellwork. When ARMY waves their light bombs in synchronization, they create an astral grid of focused intention.

Invocation Through Fan Chants: Traditional witches invoke deities. K-pop fans summon the power of their idols through meticulously timed chants. These aren't just noises, they're sonic egregores, living energy forms that strengthen the idols' presence and success. Instead of 2D pictograms, fans charge 3D performers like holographic sigils.

The Alchemy of Glamour: K-pop masters glamour magic, the ability to shift perception and embody archetypal energies. Idols undergo ritualized alchemy as they go on stage, becoming vessels for larger-than-life forces. This transformation isn't superficial. It's the same process ritual magicians have practiced for centuries, perfected and amplified through modern technology.

Choreography as Spellcasting: The synchronized movements in K-pop aren't just visually impressive. Each gesture directs energy. Each formation amplifies intention. Groups like SEVENTEEN execute patterns that mesmerize viewers energetically, not just visually. Your casual altar gestures can't compare to this level of somatic precision.

The Technical Mastery Behind Magical Results

K-pop training demands years of relentless practice, often 11+ hours daily. When INFINITE performed their trademark "knife-like" choreography, that precision comes from thousands of repetitions. Their razor-sharp movements create precise pathways for intention to manifest. This shows that technique matters.

Too many modern witches think magical aptitude is about innate talent or sensitivity. It's not. Those grimoires gathering dust? They're training manuals, not decoration. Magic isn't democratic, it's meritocratic. When you need that court case won or rent money manifested, you need magical muscle memory. You need to have done the work.

Han: The Emotional Engine Powering the Spell

K-pop has a secret weapon: Han. This uniquely Korean concept represents deep, intense emotions born from collective trauma. It fuels their magical operations. Korean culture doesn't repress these emotions; it channels them alchemically. Pain transforms into power.

Western magic often fails because practitioners fear these primal, uncomfortable forces. They bypass their shadows. They avoid their depths. Magic without emotional intensity is like a car without fuel—pretty but useless. When BTS performs, they channel collective Han. They transform inter-generational trauma into manifested reality. They move energy that's been stuck for generations.

Ancient Roots in Modern Form

What makes K-pop especially powerful is how it preserves ancient magical traditions in contemporary form. Korean shamanism (Muism) has used music, dance, and rhythmic chants to invoke spirits for millennia. The discipline of idol training parallels spiritual apprenticeship in Daoist and Buddhist temples: repetition leading to transcendence. Many idol concepts draw from traditional Asian mythologies, creating modern pantheons of living deities.

K-pop isn't breaking from history. It continues Asia's magical traditions on the global stage. These practices never died; they evolved. For witches reclaiming ancestral spiritual heritage, K-pop offers a vital bridge between past and future.

The Stakes Are Real

What makes K-pop magic so effective is precisely what most modern magical practice lacks: absolute necessity. Korean entertainment wasn't created for fun. A nation's future depended on it.

Your magical practice needs that same urgency. Climate chaos looms. Economic systems falter. Society fragments.

These aren't abstract concerns, they're immediate threats requiring high-stakes magical intervention.

Are you practicing like your survival depends on it?

Because it does.

K-pop shows that effective magic combines theatrical presence, technical mastery, emotional intensity, and collective participation, all driven by absolute necessity. Don't be a tourist in magic ... be a technician.

The world is burning down while you arrange crystals in geometric patterns. Where is your pulsating drive to slide into salvation? Put your hips into it, your blood into it, your sweat into it.

High-stakes ritual might save you. Instagram witchcraft won't.

18

My Knees Hurt Like a Village
POETRY

Gitanjali Lena

At arrivals, the flock
movements encircled feet calloused perimeter
staccatoed
the choreography of a herd

ego death by splintered coconuts
the backs of my knees opened up to a village
new roads to a heart redesigned by a cyclone

a recurring cough indicated a crone
arthritis my ancestors slowing my pace

thorn fangs pierce my crown
machetes creep upwards my shins

there's a constant ringing where I used to
pray
against a dial tone

Myth and serpents marry meaning

We didn't begin at our birthplace

19

The Girl with the Golden Hair
FICTION
Sara Surani

"You know, janan, when I was your age, I had hair just like yours."

Ajai lifts my chin and gently kisses the crown of my head, right where the gold starts to show. A tingling sensation spreads across my scalp where her lips touch. It feels like fire.

Ajai lives alone, and I have never quite understood why. We are Pakistani. We live in community, especially in Chitral. We are not meant to be alone. Yet, Ajai visits only once a year for Navroz, and we spend the day preparing samanak pudding and planting walnut and apricot trees on the farm. While my four older sisters help prepare chapshoro meat pastries, Ajai takes me to the fields. She sings to our sheep as she tills the earth, beginning in Pashto before flowing into other tongues I still do not understand. The sheep circle her, and she rises to dance, her dupatta slipping from her head onto her shoulders, revealing her golden hair beneath.

I remember the first time I saw her hair—the way it sparkled like the river when the sun kissed it.

"Ajai, there are stars on your head!" I told her one Navroz as we giggled and spun in circles beneath the sun.

She kissed the crown of my head the way she still does and whispered a prayer into my ear.

"Our heads, janan. There are stars on our heads."

I have not seen my Ajai in nearly a year, but this time, she insisted that Mumma and Baba bring me to her home the week before Navroz. She said that the two of us must spend the new year together. They wanted to resist, but they couldn't. Her eyes fired red, and that was it. I was going to spend Navroz at her little river house in Mastuj.

I have seen the fear in others' faces when Ajai's eyes burn red, but whenever she looks at me, her gaze softens. She pulls me between her legs and tells me stories as she massages apricot oil into my hair. She plaits three braids, weaving them into a master braid, then decorates it with blue poppies.

"Zma janan Azhdaha," she murmurs, her voice like an incantation. "My dear Azhdaha."

She kisses my golden roots before singing my name again.

"Today is Navroz, the beginning of the new year. I want to show you something special."

She takes my hand and leads me to the river. We sit beside the shore, her fingers still curled around mine. Closing her eyes, she begins to sing, just as she does every year with the sheep—first in Pashto, then flowing into a language I have never understood. Until now.

Her words touch my skin like wind, dancing their way inside me until I feel her rhythms pulsing in my bones. My body sways, my throat burning.

"Ajai, I feel sick," I whisper, fear welling in my eyes like tears.

I turn toward her, and her hair glows golden, like the stars.

She pulls me closer to the river, guiding my fingers

toward the water. I see my reflection—and yet, I do not recognize it.

The face I have known all my life now looks foreign. My golden hair is unbraided, wisps of stars flying in all directions. The blue poppies have fallen to my shoulders. My eyes burn like fire. Tears stream down my cheeks, leaving glowing trails in their wake.

I am beautiful.

"Ajai, I still feel sick," I tell her, the heat in my throat growing unbearable.

"Zma janan Azhdaha, sing!" My dear Azhdaha, sing!

A song erupts from my throat, my body trembling. The melody is unfamiliar, yet as the words leave my lips, I remember.

I close my eyes and see them—a circle of women with golden hair like mine, standing by the same river, their braids woven with bright blue poppies. Their chins tilt toward the sky as they sing. I see them swaying. I see them shake. And as hot tears stream down their faces, the river begins to tremble.

Thirteen dragons emerge from the water. Their iridescent blue scales shimmer as they rise, their golden manes flowing like sunlight.

Still shaking, I open my eyes.

The once-calm river now rages.

"Ajai janan," I whisper. "Am I ... a dragon?"

Her eyes glint with mischief.

"No, janan," she says, teasing. "You are not a dragon."

The water erupts before us.

"Sing, janan, keep singing!"

As my grandmother and I continue, I feel myself singing incantations across languages—Pashto, Wakhi, Baltistan, Urdu, Dari, Farsi, Khowar, Shina, Burushaski, amongst others. My body trembles, and the dragons leap from the water, soaring into the sky. Their brilliant blues and greens shimmer above me, their golden manes glimmering like stars. I recognize the mythical water dragons from the children's books I read as a child but can't quite remember the name for them. I never thought they were real.

Ajai reads my mind, her eyes never leaving the sky. "Azhdaar, janan."

They swirl and dance, playing with each other, their tails creating sparkling ripples in the clouds. When the sun kisses their skin, they sparkle. It is a sight so magnificent that I can't stop watching.

I turn to Ajai. Her eyes fire red—but I do not fear them.

They make me brave.

Her eyes are fire, but also the softest I have ever seen them.

"Azhdaha, you are a dragon keeper," she tells me, lifting my chin and kissing the crown of my head before erupting into another song.

20

An Ordinary Day in the Life of the White Snake Bai Suzhen as Ms. Lim

FICTION

Christine H. Chen

Sometimes, she just wants to shed her human skin, slide back into her true form, to scare the shit out of the jerk who cut her off on 95 South. Always abiding by the rules, she was driving within the speed limit, when his red Tesla roadster almost hit her Honda civic and made her veer to the right. As he passed her, he flipped his finger, *humans are so rude*, but not only that, it turns out he's also going to the same supermarket she's heading to, and once again, he's got the upper hand, he slides right into the spot she's planned to park, next to the entrance. She stays calm, he's not worth her bite. She's only got so much venom in her.

Besides, she's in a rush. When is she not in a rush? Her list goes on. Get groceries, drive back home, cut vegetables, marinate chicken thighs, cook the rice, feed her two children, Mei-Mei and Kuo-Kuo, help them with their math homework, rehearse her work presentation for Monday, impress the investors at the zoo, so they'll shed money to keep endangered species safe and thriving—her real families and relations—like the Golden Lanceheads, the Santa Catalina Rattlesnakes, the Wagner vipers, protect them from being poached, mangled for their organs, sold and eaten as delicatessen or as some made-up cure for male impotency.

Last time, her manager, Tom Wong, had sneered and growled, "Who cares about snakes? Abominable pests, get the money for the Panda, everyone loves pandas!" She'd pressed her jaws down for fear her fangs would rise out of frustration. *Humans are the abominable ones!* Yet, she can't imagine returning to the boredom of the Heavens where things indeed, are easier for a mythical and magical creature that she is. She can't abandon her two children after the less than amicable "divorce" with the human male she had once supposedly fallen in love with. In reality, it was the pressure that her adoptive human parents and relatives in China and America laid on her that got her to accept being married, like *every woman should* (her Ba's words) so her parents wouldn't be *losing face,* and *why would she want to be called an old maid, why was she being so selfish, and why wouldn't she want to make them happy after all the hardships they endured to adopt her after several failed attempts of having a child etc.* Being the good girl that she's always been, and desiring to honor her adoptive parents who had no inkling as to who she really is, she had agreed to date and marry a nice young man her parents had vetted, who turned out to be not nice at all, shortly after the wedding.

Now that she's made a permanent residence in the human realm, she must keep a job. She needs the dollars for the house mortgage, the car insurance that keeps increasing every year, the gas and electricity bills, the chicken eggs for Sunday brunch for her children who like cooked human food, unlike her, who still gobbles rats when she's craving for raw flesh. Everything costs so much more these days. Her pride can wait for a few years of human life.

So here she is, picking up Fuji apples from the bin when her eyes detect a movement to her left, her senses say *danger,* the man who cut her off, who took her parking spot (blue shirt open to show off curly chest hair, brown hair, too much cologne, 10 am Sunday brunch alcohol breath) brushes her rear, his hand glides in front of her to grab an apple and in its trajectory, rubs her breasts. She stands still. He smirks. Walks away, winking, with a look that says, *so what are you going to do about it?*

When she's angry, her snaky nature surges and does wonders. She flits through the aisles, her shopping is done in a whirlwind, she's at the cashier, right behind the man. She flicks her forked tongue slightly. Her sensor tells her his chemical signature. He wouldn't see it coming.

She follows him in her silver-gray Honda '98, exits at Weston, parks a few blocks away while he's pulling in his driveway with his Fuji apple and a pack of coffee. She glides around the exterior of a vast mansion with three garages, the type of home that smells of multi million dollars, maids, boats, gardeners. She scents his odor, and someone else's faint smell. No one else is at home. She slides to a large expanse of glass, peeks into a marbled kitchen and glints of stainless steel. Empty beer cans on the kitchen countertop, dirty dishes, a half full take-out container of baby clam spaghetti are thrown in the sink. Farther inside, blankets in disarray on an immense white couch in front of a glass-fronted gas chimney. The wife or a girlfriend must be away.

She rings the doorbell.

He swings open the door. "What do you want?" he says and gives her a once over, lingering on her chest, "Do I know you?" as she slips past him. He doesn't even recognize the woman he's groped.

She's disgusted by him, but her craving takes over. Her eyes shift into golden slits, and as a memory flickers in the man's mind, she sloughs off her human body; her dress tears, revealing her skin glistening with silver scales, glorious sparkles of gold and amber cut through the pale sun rays from the windows. She undulates on the fancy Brazilian wood floor towards him. His eyes bulge in horrified shock. He opens his mouth to scream but already, she's spiraling around him, she tightens, curls, tightens, curls, curls. He can't talk, can't move, can't breathe. She opens her jaw wide, slurps him down. She tastes the salt of his blood, the bitter earthiness of his muscles, his flesh, somewhat bland.

It's been a while since she's had real food. Her last meal was her ex-husband who raised his fist on her more than once.

She belches.

21

Dreams of a Large Oak Tree
NONFICTION

Sonya Rhen

My mother was born in Pusan, South Korea in 1941. (In 2000 the revised romanization officially changed the spelling to Busan.) She came to America after marrying a US Army soldier in 1966. I can't even begin to imagine how difficult it was for her to leave family, country, culture and traditions behind.

When I was five years old, my mother had a dream. She saw her mother sitting under a large oak tree. She woke up filled with sadness. She knew her mother was dying.

I don't know how she knew, but she did. Being Korean, she held a deep reverence for the interpretation of dreams. Maybe more of us would if we talked about our dreams, wrote them down and kept track of them. But living in the United States, it's not something that western cultures put much faith in.

Living in Federal Way, Washington, (halfway between Seattle and Tacoma) I'm not sure that she would have come to this conclusion so far from her native land, if she hadn't had dreams like this in the past. Maybe she dreamed about her grandmother sitting under an oak tree before she died, or her older brother. Though she would not have dreamed about her father sitting under an oak tree since he died before she was born. In fact, I was told that her name "Yu" from "Yu Suk," the Chinese character, means "born without a father." Imagine having to bear that name growing up? But that is another story.

My mother never claimed to be a shaman or wise woman. She didn't tell people she had "the sight" or anything like that. She just said, "I know things," in that way that made you feel like she knew things that most people couldn't. It was scary.

Despite her being deeply religious, or maybe because of it, she believed in the power of dreams. After all, there are a lot of dream interpretations in the Bible, but still, she didn't talk about it with a lot of people. There were stories and things that were shared with friends and acquaintances, and there were things that were never shared outside the family. Some things you just didn't talk about.

So, this was the early 1970s and long-distance phone calls overseas were expensive. After my mother had this dream, she received an airmail letter from Korea. Airmail letters for overseas were written on special blue fold up envelope paper. The paper was very thin, so it would cost less to mail. You wrote on both sides, but not the part where the address and the back of the envelope would be. The letter would be folded up in a particular manner, and you would lick the edge to seal the single page into an envelope. The front edges would have dark blue and red stripes on them. Besides being very thin and expensive to send, they also took a long time to arrive.

The delay in my mother receiving this letter from Korea telling her that her mother was sick was enough to make a significant difference. My mother called long distance as soon as she received the letter, they told her that my grandmother was very sick and only had a short time left to live.

I imagine after her dream that she knew her mother was dying. Maybe she even asked my father to buy her a plane ticket to go home. My parents were married in Korea and came to the United States in 1967 when my father left the army. Since that time, she had not been back to Korea. This was before the government deregulated the airline industry in 1978. The price of a plane ticket to Korea from Seattle was not something a newly starting out family could afford, let alone three tickets, if we all had flown. But it took some time to arrange a flight, buy a ticket, and find someone to look after a small five-year-old girl.

By the time my mother was ready to leave she received the phone call that her mother had passed away. She would not be in time to see her before she died. She would only be in time to attend the funeral. My mother had wanted to show her mother her child. That was never going to happen.

The next time my mom dreamed, she saw my dad's mother sitting under an oak tree. My father was a mechanical engineer. He was a man of science. But he was clearly shaken by my mother's dream, so he called his family home in Pennsylvania and found out that his mother was indeed sick. My mother told him he needed to go home, and he didn't argue with her. Or if he did, he didn't win the argument. He flew home, just in time to see my grandmother before she passed away.

About a decade later, my cousin and her son had stayed with us before moving to Florida. My mother had another dream, that her two-year-old great nephew had spots on his face. My mother called her niece (even though it was long-distance, but at least it wasn't overseas and we could afford it now.) She was astonished and asked my mother, "Auntie, how did you know Benji had chicken pox?"

There is a skepticism in much of western culture about things that are intangible and immeasurable. Certainly not everyone is a skeptic, but enough people are. It's good to have a healthy dose of doubt to keep us safe from scams and cons. However, when my cousin sends me a text asking me to translate a card that my mother wrote to her, and it just happens to be my birthday, I say it's a sign from my mother and not a coincidence.

I don't know if my mother had any other prophetic dreams, but it seems to have passed to my sister and I, at least a little bit. My sister told me she dreamed the sex of at least one of my children. As for me, would you believe me if I told you I dreamed about 9/11 the night before it happened?

Contributor Bios

Ai Jiang is a Chinese-Canadian writer, Ignyte, Bram Stoker, and Nebula Award winner, and Hugo, Astounding, Locus, Aurora, and BFSA Award finalist from Changle, Fujian currently residing in Toronto, Ontario. Her work can be found in F&SF, The Dark, The Masters Review, among others. She is the recipient of Odyssey Workshop's 2022 Fresh Voices Scholarship and the author of *A Palace Near the Wind, Linghun* and *I AM AI*. Find her on X (@AiJiang_), Insta (@ai.jian.g), and online (http:// aijiang.ca).

Angela Yuriko Smith is a third-generation Ryukyuan-American, award-winning poet, author, and publisher with 20+ years in newspapers. Publisher of Space & Time magazine (est. 1966), two-time Bram Stoker Awards® Winner, and HWA Mentor of the Year, she shares Authortunities, a free weekly calendar of author opportunities at authortunities.substack.com.

Arushi Karthik is a clinical researcher by day, writer by night. She lives in a small city in New England with her two dogs and anxiety. In her free time, she enjoys hiking, camping, and writing in the wilderness.

Ayida Shonibar (she/they) writes dark and wistful speculative fiction about misfits, monsters, mischief-makers. Spanning genres and age categories, their short stories, poetry, and essays appear or are forthcoming in various publications, including Silk & Sinew (Bad Hand Books), Heartlines Spec, Book XI, If There's Anyone Left, Worlds of Possibility, Wilted Pages (Shortwave Publishing), Tasavvur, and Asian Ghost Short Stories (Flame Tree Publishing), among others. Their writing has been supported by a Horror Writers Association Diversity Grant. You can find more information at ayidashonibar.com.

Benebell Wen is the author of *I Ching: The Oracle*, a translation of the Book of Changes annotated with cultural and historical references, restoring the hexagrams to their shamanic origins, and also the author of *The Tao of Craft: Fu Talismans and Casting Sigils in the Eastern Esoteric Traditions*. At www.benebellwen.com you'll be able to source dozens of free or low-cost educational multimedia courses on Eastern and Western esotericism.

Chaweon Koo is a writer of the intersection of pop culture, the occult, and futurism. Her <u>Tik Tok</u> is one of the most popular occult accounts on the platform. She also interviews some of the most distinguished occultists and witches in the English-speaking world on her podcast, "<u>Witches & Wine</u>" Her book "<u>Spell Bound: A new witch's guide to crafting the future</u>" details her journey from an atheist witch into one of the most visible East Asian practitioners of both Eastern and Western occult traditions.

Christine H. Chen was born in Hong Kong and grew up in Madagascar before settling in Boston where she worked as a research chemist. Her fiction has appeared in *The Pinch, Fractured Lit., Atticus Review, Bending Genres, Time & Space Magazine,* and other journals and anthologies. Her work was selected for inclusion in *Wigleaf Top 50 Very Short Fictions 2023, Best Microfiction 2024, 2025, Best Small Fictions 2024,* and has won prizes in the *Fractured Lit. Anthology Prize 2023,* the *SmokeLong Grand Micro 2024.* She is a recipient of the 2022 Mass Cultural Council Artist Fellowship and the co-translator from French of the hybrid novel *My Lemon Tree* (Spuyten Duyvil, 2023). Find her stories at www.christinehchen.com

Frances Lu Pai Ippolito (she/her) is a Chinese American judge, mom, writer, and publisher in Portland, Oregon. Her writing has appeared in several venues including Nightmare Magazine, Flame Tree's Asian Ghost Stories, Chromophobia, Mother: Tales of Terror and Love, and Unquiet Spirits. She is the founder of game and book publisher Demagogue Press and the award-winning nonprofit, Qilin Press, which focuses on community stories. She is also the co-editor of two cozy horror anthologies through Underland Press, and serves as a HWA Trustee. But most importantly, she believes in ghosts. IG: @demagogue_press & @qilin_press

Gitanjali Lena is a non-binary queer disabled playwright, poet, and comic with Tamil/Sinhalese ancestry living in T'karonto. They co-founded the Teardrop Collective for South Asian queer and trans theatre artists. *Leopards & Peacocks*, a comedy, is their first play. Their writing appears in Fireweed Feminist Quarterly, the Whose Your Daddy Queer Parenting Anthology, Parallel Tracks 2.0, Hir Magazine, and the Maza Collective Digital Anthology. Gitanjali attended the Banff Centre Poetry Residency in 2023. Gitanjali has entertained audience for the New Normal, Buddies Pride Cabaret, and the International Festival of Authors with the Tam Fam Lit Jam in 2022 and 2024.They are an Amma & community elder aging disgracefully enacting a cultural intifada with their first collection of poetry *Overgrowth; the understory*.

Mudang Jenn is a shaman, ritual tender, and teaching artist uncovering the hidden energies within, awakening the body as both vessel and drum for spirit and ancestral memory. With roots as a traditionally initiated mudang and her lived experience navigating life as a diasporic shaman, she creates ceremonial spaces that honors ancestral traditions while confronting personal healing, transformation, and collective remembrance. A radical remembering of our bodies as sacred shindanji (신단지, spirit jars)—vessels holding the energies of spirit that move within, around, and through us. By awakening the body as a drum, we call power into form, sound, and movement.

Mudang Jenn has taught, performed, and shared her ritual work at institutions including RISD (Rhode Island School of Design), Columbia Theological Seminary, Recess Art, Creative Time, The Nicholson Project, and Canal Projects NYC. Her work has also contributed to academic research, appeared in published research, and been presented at anthropology conferences.

Her work and story have been featured in pop culture and media outlets including HuffPost and Popdust.

Kristy Park Kulski is a Hawaii-born Korean-American author, historian, and career vampire of patriarchal tears. Channeling a lifelong obsession with history and the morose she's managed to birth the gothic horror novel, *Fairest Flesh*, and novella, *House of Pungsu*, and is the editor of the Asian-diaspora folk-horror anthology, *Silk & Sinew*. She bartered nine years of her life to the U.S. Navy and Air Force for food and later taught college history for a captive audience. Trapped by a force field, she currently resides in the woods of Northeast Ohio where she (probably) brews potions and talks to ghosts. Follow her on Bluesky @garnetonwinter or garnetonwinter.com.

Lee Murray ONZM is a writer, editor, poet and screenwriter from Aotearoa New Zealand, a Shirley Jackson Award and five-time Bram Stoker Award® winner. A *USA Today* bestselling author with more than forty titles to her credit, she holds a New Zealand Prime Minister's Award for Literary Achievement in Fiction, the first author of Asian descent to achieve this, and is an Honorary Literary Fellow of the New Zealand Society of Authors. Her latest work, NZSA Cuba Press Prize-winner *Fox Spirit on a Distant Cloud*, was released in 2024 from The Cuba Press. Read more at leemurray.info

M. S. Marquart (she/her) is a disabled, mixed-race Asian American, diasporic Korean American and German American poet. Her writing explores the impacts of chronic illness, disability, and the issues that intersect with them, and seeks to shed light on the hidden daily lives of people living with Long COVID and myalgic encephalomyelitis (ME or ME/CFS), many of whom are primarily homebound like her and therefore missing from society.

Her work has been published or is forthcoming in *Kaleido-scope: Exploring the Experience of Disability through Literature and the Fine Arts; Lombardi Voices; FLARE Magazine; Wishbone Words; miniMAG; Micromance Magazine; I'll Get Right On It: Poems on Working Life in the Climate Crisis,* which is a publication by the Land and Labour Poetry Collective, and *Pillow Writers Anthology 2*, which is a publication by the #MEAction online writers group for writers with Long Covid and/or ME/CFS. You can find her at https://msmarquart.com or instagram @m_s_marquart

Pauline Chow is a writer, coach, and ancestral magic practitioner, crafting alternative histories and optimistic futures. Not your average data scientist, she once sued slumlords and advocated for affordable housing in Southern California. She is a Pushcart Prize nominated author with words in Cosmic Monthly Horror, Space and Time Magazine, Apocalypse Confidential, and more. Her gothic fantasy, Chasing Moonflowers, is one of Kirkus Reviews' September 2024 indie book recommendations. Connect with her on www.paulinechowstories.com or @paulinechow.bsky.social.

Dr. Wuwong (PhD in biochemistry, MBA in finance) has published 120+ scientific books and papers (under her legal name) and a few fiction books under **R. F. Whong**. She lives in the Midwest with her husband, a retired pastor. They served together at three churches from 1987 to 2020. She is a 2025 Featured Author by the Minnesota Anoka County Library.

Sam Wilket (she/her) writes strange, surreal, and sometimes scary stories. She is a second-generation Canadian of white British/Chinese descent, and is currently based in Toronto. She also runs *Forests in Her Mind*, a newsletter where she recommends stellar speculative fiction by women authors. Find out more at samwilket.com

Sara Surani is a writer, activist, entrepreneur, educator, researcher, and co-founder of She is the Universe - a global movement for girls' empowerment. She has lived and worked all over the world, bridging storytelling with gender equity, health advocacy, and education, from fishing towns in Tanzania to the depths of the Amazon jungle. Sara works with community empowerment and entrepreneurship globally, collaborating with grassroots and governments across the US, Asia, Africa, and Latin America. She believes that stories move people and have the power to change the world. A daughter of Pakistani-Muslim immigrants in South Texas, Sara holds degrees from Harvard University and Tsinghua University. She is a Fulbright Fellow and a Schwarzman Scholar, and is always looking for an excuse to learn a new language. Her first collection of poetry and prose, Songs of My Grandmother, is now available in stores everywhere. Sara finds home in many people and places, and is currently finding home in New York City. www.sarasurani.com.

Sobhia Kamal Jamro is a writer from Karachi, currently pursuing an MFA Writing at The New School as a Fulbright Scholar. Her work is about her heritage and identity as a Sindhi Pakistani. When not writing, she daydreams and takes long walks and talks to trees as if they're real people.

Sonya Rhen is the author of the *Shredded Orphans* series of humorous science fiction novels, as well as short stories, romance and poetry. She lives in the Pacific Northwest with her husband and two children. They share their home with an anxious but clever dog. She loves things that make her laugh and is always on the lookout for the perfect French Dip sandwich. When she's not writing you might find her dancing.

T. S. Ren is a writer born and raised in New York by a collective of resilient Chinese women. She works in book publishing, and is passionate about championing authors who dream of ways to make our society more equitable. In her free time, she enjoys crafting book earrings, learning about deep sea creatures, and wandering NYC with her loved ones.

Theresa Drew Falk is a Filipina writer and educator who has taught English and Women's Studies for thirty years. Her poetry and prose have appeared in various publications, and her most recent work is included in *Nonwhite and Woman: 131 Micro Essays on Being in The World*, a 2023 Independent Publisher Book Award winner, through Woodhall Press. Theresa lives with her family in Honolulu, Hawaii, where she is working on a memoir about motherhood and adoption.

Wen Wen Yang is a Chinese American from the Bronx, New York. She graduated from Barnard College of Columbia University with a degree in English and creative writing. You can find her short fiction in Fantasy Magazine, Apex, Cast of Wonders and more. An up-to-date bibliography is on WenWenWrites.com.

Acknowledgments

Thank you to those who have come before us; those who knew, who dared, who did and who have been kept silent. May we all find our voices, our words and our coven. Thank you for walking the pathless path with us, and for Lee Murray and Geneve Flynn for taking the first steps.

Thanks to everyone who believes in the anthology, trusting Angela and I with your words. Being able to bring this idea together in such a short period of time is nothing less than astonishing. Community makes this life a little bit sweeter and writing a lot less lonely.

Also from the Publishers

Authortunities Press

- Tortured Willows: Bent. Bowed. Broken.
- Inujini

Ghastly Goings-On Press

- Chasing Moonflowers: A Gothic Historical Fantasy
- Goodnight Nobody: and other haunted bedtime stories